*What We Come in For*

# *What We Come in For*

STORIES BY

Richard Lundquist



*University of Missouri Press*
*Columbia and London*

University of Missouri Press, Columbia, Missouri 65201
Printed and bound in the United States of America

5 4 3 2 1 04 03 02 01 00

Library of Congress Cataloging-in-Publication Data

Lundquist, Richard, 1957–
What we come in for : stories / by Richard Lundquist.
p. cm.
ISBN 0-8262-1270-0 (alk. paper)
1. United States—Social life and customs—20th century—Fiction.
I. Title.
PS3562.U548 W47 2000
813'.6—dc21 00-020453

∞™ This paper meets the requirements of the
American National Standard for Permanence of Paper
for Printed Library Materials, Z39.48, 1984.

Designer: Stephanie Foley
Cover design: Vickie Kersey DuBois
Typesetter: BookComp, Inc.
Printer and binder: Thomson-Shore, Inc.
Typefaces: Frutiger and ITC Giovanni

"Silence and Slow Time" first appeared in *Kansas Quarterly;* "The Motions of Love" in the *High Plains Literary Review;* "Dust Devils" in the *Colorado North Review;* "The Greener Pasture" in *Talking River Review;* and "Now It Looks Respectable" and "The Flood" in *Cold Drill.*

*For my mother and father—*
*she, who believed that every-*
*thing should be just so—*
*and he, who yearned.*

# Contents

# *What We Come in For*

*Everything we own has brought us here: from here we speak.*

William Stafford
"Lake Chelan"

# A Town, Paradise, Was Built

*Down there, in the heartland, lies a grid of common roads seen from above if seen at all as a sturdy quilt or a worn linoleum floor, broken here and there by dark clusters of foliage stretched like a tent over the small towns, buttressed by the bone-white grain elevators and church steeples.*

*Away from those towns, across the fields, runs a river, like a crack in a pane of glass, bending and winding until it swells into a reservoir as blue as the evening sky. In the harvested fields the laggard smoke and dust from a tractor converge, cattle wedge out into the rolling grasslands or crowd into the grid of corrals, and on the silver highways the cars and trucks flee the common land.*

*Down there, when it was called Quivira, in 1541, Francisco Vasques de Coronado stood atop the bluff overlooking one of those rivers, gazed across the land the natives called paradise, searched the grassy hills to the north, the clustered cottonwoods in the lowlands of the east, the dark river and the high, flat plateau in the south, the withers-high prairie through which he had traveled the last nine months, and understood, finally, he had been led astray.*

*There were no thick-walled cities of gold, no El Dorado of the plains, no crowned ruler to welcome him, just the tiny grass-thatched lodges with the smoke of dung rising through a hole in their roofs; and a tattooed and nearly naked Wichita chief, who, like the Pawnee guide, the Turk, kept pointing Coronado north. Away.*

*Away to the promised land. Cibola. Away.*

*So his guide, the Turk, was made to kneel, pray for his immortal soul, then beheaded on the south slope of the bluff that centuries later would bear his name, although by then no one would know why.*

*Three hundred years later the immigrants returned, again with Bibles, but this time in lieu of the sword they brought plows and oxen, seed wheat and corn, barley and oats, and barbed wire.*

*The land was sectioned off.*

*Quartered.*

*Plowed.*

*Planted, and in the valley of the Quivira River below Turk's Bluff, a town, Paradise, was built, not because that's what it was but because that's what they hoped it would become. They endured under a vast empty sky more terrifying than the bursts of thunder, lightning, tornadoes, dust storms, locusts—and the wind, always the wind—that came to fill it.*

*They hunkered down, drilled their wells deep, dug out their homes, tap-rooted their lives.*

*Down there, in the heartland, in that land of silence, it was what they came in for.*

# Silence and Slow Time

*I remember this, still.* At dusk, I first saw the mouse-man come up the road; his car shimmered and rattled in the dim light, slowing as it got to our driveway. Then I lost sight of it as a balloon of dust caught it and swallowed it. Yet when the dust passed, it was still there. Finally it poked its grille into our drive, and ascended the sloping hill to our house. I watched the dust move on past the drive, down the road until it dissolved and fell. So much dust was unusual in the fall, but the dust was tough and enduring—I'd heard men say that—and even the recent rain could not control it. When the mouse-man stopped his car in our yard, a balloon smaller than the first blew past him and made me sneeze. My father used to say he believed I was allergic to dust, and wasn't that a heckuva note for a farm kid.

I waved my hand to clear the air before my face and saw the mouse-man step from his car and talk to my mother. He looked like others she had hired. His khaki pants were baggy, soiled with sweat and oil, and his shirt was the same, a patchwork of browns so that it seemed he wore a uniform. His face was dark and jagged; then white and smooth like mine. It changed one to the other, then back as I watched, as if played upon by the diminishing light. I wanted to reach out, touch it, find out which it was, but I caught myself. On his face was a gray mustache, and above it his large nose twitched in the air. He was unkempt, except for the hair. The few gray strands of it were neatly combed, streaked atop his head like the shadow of a grasping hand.

"Is that your boy?" he asked.

"Will," my mother said. "Little Will," and the mouse-man said I looked as if I would be a big help to him. He bowed his head and spat into the dust. The tobacco juice bubbled up and then settled into mud. He eyed it for awhile, then kicked some dirt over it.

"You know much 'bout workin' yet?" He tilted his head toward me. His voice was authoritative, and I felt accused. I curled my toes in my shoes and pushed my voice out, making it sound like his.

"Some, but I guess I could learn some more."

The mouse-man smoothed the dirt with his boot, then smiled as if he saw something pleasing in the formation. "Hold it," he said, and moved toward his car. He reached in the front seat and came out with something. He threw it at me. I grabbed for it, but it slithered through my fingers. I picked it up from the ground and began brushing off the dust. It was a Hershey bar.

"It's awright. A little dirt never hurt nobody."

I thanked him and looked to my mother for an objection. She made none that I could see, so I ate the bar. Then she and the mouse-man went inside, and I could see them through the kitchen window, drinking coffee and talking business. I knew she would hire him. Since my father passed away, she had needed someone to feed the cattle. And mouse-men came cheap.

I finished the candy bar and went to the pump. I filled the cup and washed out the remaining sweetness of the bar. I swished the water around in my mouth and spit it out until the blackness was gone and my spit was clear again. Then I looked up at the window. My mother was gone now. Only the mouse-man remained, framed by the window like a portrait. His still, dark profile made me shake. I stepped forward but lost the focus. His lines grew blurred, dirty. I squeezed shut my eyes and whispered a prayer for a cleaner mouse-man.

The next morning the mouse-man brought me another Hershey bar.

"Here," he said. "You'll need some energy, risin' and shinin' like you are."

A part of me hesitated, though my hand moved forward to accept the bar. I knew my mother wouldn't approve so early in the day, but before I realized it I had told him thanks a million and was eating the chocolate.

He laughed and playfully messed my hair. I thought of the dirt and grease on his hands, but then I could feel the warm blood beating through the calluses and I felt strangely comforted.

"C'mon, boy. We better git a move on. You stand there much longer and I swear you're gonna grow roots."

I nodded and gulped down the rest of the bar as we climbed into the cab of the truck.

I was his right-hand man, he said, and I liked the sound of that. It ran musically from ear to ear, like the intoned reverence I heard each Sunday in church: *. . . and in Jesus Christ, his only son our Lord . . . who sitteth on the right hand of God the Father Almighty. . . .*

"Sure as hell," he laughed, hitting the brakes, "you're my right-hand man."

When he hit the brakes, it was my cue to leap from the truck and open the gate. Soon I was driving the truck. The mouse-man would shove the truck into gear and yell at me to slide my ass over. Then he bailed out on the run like a paratrooper and struggled to crawl in back. While I guided, he threw off bales of hay to the cattle. After a time I made a game of it and would begin counting when the mouse-man barked his command . . . *1* . . . *2* . . . *3* . . . *4* . . . *5* . . . I counted until I heard the first bale thud against the ground. One day we did it in three seconds, and the mouse-man said we were a hell of a team. "Yes sirree," he said, "a helluva team."

In the corral, steers lowered their heads, feigned charges, but the mouse-man always held his ground. Once, he dropped to his knees, bellowed and crawled toward a steer. The steer, hooves planted wide apart, tilted its head and snorted as it eyed the man-bull with astonishment. The mouse-man pawed at the dirt and crawled closer. Safe in the truck I wondered who would turn chicken. When they were nose to nose, the mouse-man's lips tightened and his head moved like a slingshot pulled back by an invisible, almighty hand, steadied—aimed then snapped loose and fired a plug of tobacco smack into the steer's eye. It bawled and fled, twisting and shaking its head at the ground as its haunches flew at the sky.

*Right-hand man,* I thought, *Yes sirree*! And something like sunshine was in my blood.

When the steer stopped and turned its head its eyes were like stale puddles of water. The mouse-man turned his back, hitched up his pants.

"You can bet your brown ass we're a helluva team," he said.

On cold mornings, when the truck moaned to start beneath his hands, the mouse-man and I sat in the cab and talked as men. He would shiver, breathing puffs like dust and say how cold it was, and I would say how rough it was on a man. Then he would take out his bottle and say how much a man needed something to warm himself. He would pat the bottle on its fullest part; then drink and sigh. At first I was hesitant; I felt an accomplice to some act of sin. But then I would eat my Hershey bar—my snort, he called it against my mother's wishes, and taste the sweetness in the sin.

He moved darkly through my thoughts that winter. At night in bed I prayed for him. I asked God to clean him up, to shower him and scrub him down with His gracious soap, to cleanse him of his sinful smell, so that I might draw near him, freely. Yet when I saw him the next morning, I was glad he was as I remembered him. This confused me, and soon my prayers became dutiful. I drifted in and out of sleep, losing the thread of my prayer. I felt guilty then, so I began to make fewer requests of God. I prayed mostly for Him to forgive the mouse-man's profanity, to take the starch out of his words, as my mother said. When the mouse-man swore, it did not sound like the idle profanities of other men. When the mouse-man cursed, it shook the sky, like a thunderstorm.

"Goddamnit," he raged at me, whenever I refused to enter the feed shed. His words felt like the claws of the rat, scratching into my heart. I felt it all when he swore: the movement of my cuff and the digging claws climbing my leg, how I dropped the grain sack and clutched at the lump in my pants. Squeezing, I tried to murder the movement. Yet the strong claws kept reaching, digging toward my heart, trying to pierce it, make it bleed. I fled from the darkened shed, toward the sunlight, and squeezed harder. My hand grew damp from the blood of the rat, yet I delighted in the squeezing, the ridding of the influence, the purification. Finally I stopped running and released my grasp. The rat slid back down my leg and dropped to the ground, dead. I kicked it out of sight and turned away. For a long time then

I walked around in the sunlight, trying to warm myself and still the cold shaking of my soul.

"You goddamn little coward," he would yell at me. "You're scared to go into that shed, aren't you?" Then he would stomp with fire in his boots over to the shed and get whatever it was he wanted. Later, as we sat in the truck, there was a wound in his voice.

"You gotta have the gumption to stick your cheek out at what scares you," he said, his nose twitching. "A man's gotta be able to jump into the slop with the hogs ever now and then, or half his life gonna go right on by him. And you ain't gonna find a man around to back you up, neither, no sirree. The only one backin' you up is gonna be so far back of you that you ain't even gonna be able to see his shadow." He paused, then spit out the window in disgust. "Oh, hell," he finally said, "what's the use of one man telling another what's best."

When the mouse-man talked like that, it confused me. And in the confusion I grew angry and sullen and asked God to forgive him. His face darkened, and I saw him as a rat, menacing me. I hated him, and the more I hated him, the more he overwhelmed me. My senses sharpened, and I could hear his teeth chattering, and smell the stench of the shed on his skin. I pressed against the door of the truck. The seat put me too close to him. I was afraid he would reach over and poke me, as he did sometimes in play, and I wanted to escape. When we stopped for the gate I leaped from the truck and raced to open it. As I ran I felt free again, and when I returned to the truck he always seemed changed. His nose was still again, his face white, and the harsh lines had run from his face like tears.

"Someday," he sighed, "you're goin' to raise hell and be goddamn glad you did."

But the authority had gone out of his voice, and he seemed free of some burden. He laughed, and his voice flowed smoothly again into my ears. I wanted to reach out and catch it in my hands and spread it over his face like butter on bread. But I didn't dare.

When spring came, the mouse-man would vanish for two or three days at a time. My mother would make arrangements with a neighbor to do the work and warn me about the mouse-man. Men get restless in the spring, she said, and when the cattle were gone, the mouse-man too would be gone. She didn't have to tell me that, I could feel it in the mornings when the mouse-man would not come.

I would awake early on those mornings and lie in bed and watch the rising sun. I knew the mouse-man would not be coming. When the sun turned from orange to yellow, I would peel the winter blankets off, one by one, until only the sheet covered me. Under the veil my body looked like the trunk and branches of a winter tree. I watched it to see if it would grow in the new sunlight like a plant. The mouse-man had told me that if you awake early enough you can catch with your eyes the growth of your very own body. It grows only at night, he said, because then your guard is down, and you dream dreams so exciting that your body quivers like water in the wind. Everything happens when it's least expected, he said, so I lay there, trying hard not to expect my body to grow. I clenched my fists in concentration; the vessels in my temples swelled under the strain. I squinted my eyes—and listened.

Then I heard it. I heard the deep rumbling of my body growing. I opened my eyes. I studied the length of my body carefully. My eyes rolled down it from my chest to my toes. But it looked the same to me. I studied the creases in the sheets, and I could see that my toes reached to the same crease as before. Then my stomach growled like a grinder, and I knew for certain that the mouse-man had lied to me. He's wrong; he's telling me a story. I laughed at the news. The mouse-man is wrong, I sang. I laughed in the warmth of the room; then it turned to a giggle and got out of control. I kicked off the sheet and flopped in bed like a fish until my breath failed and I felt dead and light as the sun-sparkled motes in my room.

When the mouse-man returned, his face looked gnawed by lack of sleep. Whiskers pierced his cheeks and chin, and his hair bristled unkempt in the breeze like a tumbleweed. I looked up into his eyes, but they were lost above me. When I walked beside him I smelled the liquored musk of his flesh. We walked toward the barn in silence. He seemed unwilling to speak, and I was unable. The lump in my stomach had worked up to my throat, and lodged there. Finally I could not stand it any longer. I gathered the words together in my chest and pushed them out.

"Do you figure we got time for a snort today?"

A tired smile curled around his lips as he raised his head.

"Yeah, maybe you and me will find time to have a snort when we're through."

But his eyes were following the cattle truck as it idled up the driveway, circled, and stopped with the hiss of air brakes. The mouse-man motioned it back to the loading chute, and then the driver, a quick, lean man with a sleeveless T-shirt, hopped down and rolled up the doors to the silver trailer.

In the loading pens, amidst the swirling dust and clanging gates, the mouse-man skirted the bawling herd, then darted in and out of pockets of cattle, driving them up the chute and finally out of sight through the gaping doors of the truck. I stood on the fence of the chute and poked a stick into their backs, forcing them upward. In the thick dust I would lose sight of the mouse-man. But then I would hear his voice and his whip cracking like lightning.

"Git up you son of a bitch, git up there," he sang.

And I joined in, his right-hand man, prodding and singing along with the mouse-man.

"Git up you son of a bitch, git up there."

The fury of noise was like the wild rumblings I heard in the mornings in the sunlight of my room. The mix of dust and manure hung in the air for a long time after the last steer was loaded, and we were silent and tired and happy.

When I climbed down from the fence, I looked down at my hands and my clothes. They were dirty and sweat-stained like a man's—like a mouse-man's. I sighed and turned to the mouse-man.

"Well, I guess that just about does it."

The mouse-man laughed and put his arm on my shoulder as we walked. "Yes," he drawled, "that just about does it all right. You feel like havin' that snort now?"

"Hell, we might as well," I said.

The driver hopped up into the cab, leaned across the seat, and then emerged with some papers in one hand and a bottle in the other. On his left biceps a snake writhed with the flex of the muscle, hissing something I could not read. The mouse-man signed the papers and then took a drink from the bottle.

"What the hell *is* this?" He spit.

The driver laughed. "Ever taste anything like that before?"

"Hell, no! But then I ain't never tasted horse piss neither."

"What you feel burning in your heart right now, my friend, is Mexican whiskey."

"*Mexican* whiskey?"

"Yep. I bring some back ever time I make a run down into old Mexico."

"Well, I'll be damned," the mouse-man said. "I'll be damned."

"It's cheap down there, real cheap. Tell you what I'll do, friend. I'll put you on my list and bring you back enough to last 'til next Christmas. It'll run you only about . . . hell, I'll give it to you for a dollar-fifty a bottle. That includes my own handling charge."

"Shit," the mouse-man spit. "I've got a gal in town that can git me Uncle Sam's whiskey cheaper 'an that."

"That wouldn't be Marge now, would it?"

The mouse-man laughed; then his voice trailed off. He cocked his head and squinted through one eye at the driver. "You know Marge too?"

"Hell, Jesus Christ hisself has knowed Marge."

The mouse-man laughed at this and kept drinking. They talked of Marge and other things I did not understand, about distance to market, shrinkage, prices in Omaha, St. Joe, and Kansas City. I watched the mouse-man drink and wondered why he drank the Mexican whiskey if he did not like it. I felt uncomfortable, that I shouldn't be there, yet wanted very much to be there. I listened for a chance to enter their circle. I wanted to speak like them, yet I felt guilty for this desire, as their talk frightened and enticed me. I resented being shut off from them, and I puzzled as to why I wanted to be a part of something so distasteful. I spit into the dirt and watched the saliva dissolve. I kicked some dirt over it and smoothed out the formation with my boot. I tried to leave the ground looking unmarked by my boot, but finally I gave that up as hopeless. I thought of my candy bar and hoped the mouse-man would fetch it so I might join them. But he'd forgotten about me. I wanted to get it myself but decided that wouldn't be right either. I didn't know what to do, so I began to kick a hole in the ground with my boot heel. I jabbed it in the ground repeatedly, trying to make a neat hole. But the sides kept caving in, and the dust puffed up from the ground. Then I heard the driver address me.

"How 'bout the boy there? Does he want a snort too?"

I looked up from my project. I realized he was talking to me. Both he and the mouse-man were looking at me. Their heads loomed over their shoulders and above me, distorted as in a carnival mirror. My senses grew hard. I stammered under the threat, not knowing what to say. I waited and hoped the mouse-man would take up the extended bottle. The driver shook the bottle; the liquor splashed against its sides, burning deep red in the bottle. I waited for the mouse-man's hand to wrap around it. But I didn't see it, and when I looked up again he was smiling down upon me.

"I—I'm not thirsty." I finally said.

"Not thirsty?" The driver bellowed with laughter. "Hell, every man's got a thirst."

I felt the rage and indignation swelling in my face. I looked to the mouse-man for protection, but he was laughing too. I clenched my fist to fasten me in place, hold me from fleeing. I looked for something to say, something that would make me grow, and them shrink. I lowered my head, but I could still see their faces reflecting in the bottle above me. I muttered for God to give me strength and to forgive them their sins. Yet, as I prayed, I felt my hand moving to the bottle. The mouse-man had touched my hand, yet the impetus came from some part of me I didn't recognize. It wrapped around the bottle.

The bottle was cold on my lips, but the liquor flashing into my mouth stung like thorns on my tongue and throat. Against my own hand I tried to push it out, force it away, but my own hand wouldn't obey until it began shaking, and then liquor streaked down my chin like warm blood and I coughed and panted.

Finally my breathing slowed and I could feel my heart slowing too. I felt my face; it was flushed with shame and liquor and a strange satisfaction. I looked into the mouse-man's eyes. They seemed glazed with contentment. It grew silent, and I felt awkward and confused but secure too in the silence. Then a voice said *do you want to see the damnedest sight you ever saw, the damnedest sight* it said, and I thought it was the mouse-man's voice but it came from me and the words found ears and it was too late because the words found ears and then the mouse-man was again in the lead and the driver was following and they slouched like somnolent shadows in the slow silence of a dream toward the feed shed and my feet led me to follow.

The mouse-man said something and the driver said something else and then the driver said *five dollars, five dollars* the driver said, and the mouse-man said *you're on,* and they both laughed, and I could say nothing. I could only watch. They gestured slowly, lazily like scarecrows only half-alive and their mouths flapped emphatically though soundlessly. They grew darker and danced and spun incongruous pirouettes in the shadow of the shed and gestured skyward with their arms, leaping into the air and there hanging in soporific suspension for long moments like blackened motes until the mouse-man flung the bottle into the air and swept his hand to the door. My eyes floated in a daze from the bottle to the door.

He shook open the door and dust descended from the door and engulfed him in a haze; then it cleared and I could see the inside of the shed where a small light filtered through the dust to the interior and through the light I saw mice teeming throughout the interior boiling up as in a pot then settling and scurrying for cover. The mouse-man floated over the opening and blocked the light so the doorway turned black again and all I could see was his dark back disappearing into the darkness and he was gone forever. The shed shook and moaned, coughing dust from its sides and faraway I heard the driver laughing above the din in the shed and his laughter went up in puffs, drifting skyward, mixing and dissolving with moans from the shed. Then the darkened doorway turned again into the mouse-man who crawled forward on all fours, the shape of a rat, and he looked at me and his teeth chattered and mice fell from his eyes and mouth and ears and from the pores of his body and I could not run nor could I break the spell because I did not know where or how because before me stood the rat and I could not look nor could I move my eyes so I squeezed my eyes and shut my eyes and took shelter there and there I went deep inside myself and resided there and deep inside myself there I called him a sinner and there my rage waited for God to avenge it.

# Windsickness

*On the bluff above the sod house, two Lakota warriors, far from the Black Hills, reined up and let their horses nose the grass. In sacks tied to their waists were prairie turnips, which they would trade for the Wasichu's sugar. The wind blew their hair from their shoulders, tousled the manes of their horses and carried strange new odors. The ground was wet from the storm of the previous night and the clay soil of a plowed field clung to the horses' hooves.*

*As they were about to start down the bluff, a pale woman in a white apron burst from the sod house, cradling clothes and dishes and cherished possessions in her arms. She ran south into the wind, shrieking like a crow as she flung milk pans and sheets and a clock and a sack of flour into the wind until she'd rid herself of it all, and then fell or dove into the ground beside the plowed field, where she lay sobbing with her arms spread as if trying to gain purchase. Even then the wind played with her hair.*

*It was the wind that made her sick, the incessant, soundless wind that shredded her clothes on the line, dried and silted her cooling bread, tangled her hair; and then at noon her husband, his shirt and suspenders stained with sweat and the chaff of grass in his beard and hair had come in from turning the sod and said* thank God, thank God Almighty for the coolin' breeze or a man would hardly stand a chance.

*On the bluff above the homestead, the Lakota glanced at one another, nudged their horses in silence, and began their retreat north up the bluff, trying, as they vanished from the prairie, to reckon what they'd seen with the great mystery.*

# The Motions of Love

Shirley is the dancing woman. The dance began five months ago in church, but it wasn't until she took the dance home, to her kitchen in the solitude of midnight, when the house was clean and she could hear her husband Gil's troubled snoring from the distant bedroom, that the dance became a nightly ritual, and sometimes a dance of grace. At first it was a frantic dance of exorcism, but that has yielded to something more fluent, and on some nights, when she is lucky, it all comes together in a swaying fever of motion, a motion something like love, that transports her from the kitchen floor, lifts her ethereally like the angels she imagined in Sunday school as a child. Afterward she can sleep, sleep the way she had when she was first married and Gil would breathe softly in her ear on the pillow beside her head.

But tonight sleep seems hours away; her feet feel heavy as she raises her eyes to the window and a reflection of a face that looks almost pretty in the dim light. The darkness obscures the strain that shows in the daytime, when her face looks stricken, like the dried, curled leaves of the walnut tree in the backyard. Sometimes she will pause before the window or the mirroring oven door to shape her fingers into a spatula to press the flesh from her jaws into the cavity of her cheeks. But there is never enough loose flesh there, no material for molding and filling her concave cheeks. Her shoulders, too, she thinks, are too thin and her hips too large, and even her blue eyes, which shine with the clarity of the full moon when she dances, look dull and eclipsed in the daylight.

A pleasing melody comes from the radio, the promise of beginnings. She feels the music first in her hips, then her knees loosen, and her feet begin to seek in the rhythm of the dance the motion of love that is now of her own making.

As she sways, her housecoat opens where a dangling thread remains from the button that was ripped away. On her stomach the smooth scar undulates with the motion of her hips, healing finally into a soft, pink hue like a baby's skin—so unlike the rough, brittle ridge that Newhart explored with his fingers, explored as if blindfolded, explored as if deciphering a code from an alien world. Now, the only guilt she feels is that she allowed him to touch her scar. Sometimes a scar was the most sacred thing in a marriage. The most intimate.

She covers the opening with her hand, presses her palm against her stomach, but already the memory has intruded upon the perfect union of melody and muscle and flesh.

She falters outside the music, outside the moment. Her body feels heavy, weighted with a memory that settles beneath her heart.

"Paring knife slipped," she had told the doctor the day after Gil had come home drunk and surly: and when they argued about who had forsaken whom in their marriage he had grabbed for her arm and when she twisted and pulled away his wedding ring had caught her housecoat and ripped out the button.

*Look what you've done,* she said. *Just look what you've done now!* When she felt the thin, burning line on her stomach and saw the evidence of blood on Gil's wedding ring, a horror came into her eyes that could not be voiced. She stammered and pointed at the ring while Gil just stood there stupefied and awed at what he had done.

*You!* she finally said. *You!* before fleeing to the bedroom and closing the door.

The rest of the night she lay on her stomach, refusing to cry, a strip of gauze pressed between her stomach and the bed sheet, but the bleeding seeped through to the sheet, and in the morning, while breakfast was cooking, she doused the small stain with Clorox again and again before finally giving up and throwing the sheets away. Gil ate his bacon and eggs and said nothing about her injury or, for that matter, the soiled sheets. It served him right that she had burned the bacon, she thought, as it crunched noisily between his teeth. For two weeks they hardly spoke until the Saturday night when Gil came home from town with a set of new sheets for the bed, and even though they were the wrong color, Shirley put them on anyway, and that night, Gil complimented her on supper, and their lives returned to normal.

The new sheets had been washed and stacked in the closet and her wound had turned into a scar when she drove into town with the box of clothes to donate to the church. It was the middle of March, and the brown grass in the churchyard was greening at the crowns.

Along the sidewalk leading to the church basement a few crocuses had poked through the damp ground beside the low shrubs that were still brown from the hard winter. The air smelled dank and heavy; the earth held too much water, with no place for it to go. The back door of the church was unlocked so Shirley carried the box of old clothing down the stairs into a damp, dimly lit hallway where plaster crumbled from the walls.

At the bottom of the stairs she turned into the kitchen where her mother and grandmothers and other church women had arranged pies and salads and beans and potatoes for potluck dinners when she was a child. She had not been in this kitchen since her wedding reception, fifteen years ago. The long, wooden table was bare now, except for a half-empty bottle of Mogen David and a red-stained chalice beside a tray of white wafers. It was like a still life, a scene she remembered from her childhood, and she remembered too how she was unable to reconcile what was holy in the sanctuary with what was common in the kitchen. The box of clothes felt heavy in her hands, so she slid it onto the table beside the Mogen David and turned to the door.

She heard footsteps coming down the cement stairs, light, quick steps like a child's. So large and so quiet was the church that the noise startled her. She heard the squeak of tennis shoes on the cement floor as a man in a jogging suit pivoted in the doorway. He stopped quickly when he saw her.

"A visitor!" he said. "I thought I heard someone enter. I was up in my study working on next Sunday's sermon."

"The back door was unlocked, so I just came on in," Shirley explained. She gestured toward the box of clothes. "I had some clothes I cleaned out of the closet at home. They still have some use in them."

Newhart recovered and smiled professionally as he entered the kitchen. At Shirley's side he reached into the box of clothes and pulled up blouses, skirts, a dress shirt of Gil's that had never been worn, a pair of trousers that looked new.

"These are all like new," he said. "Are you sure you want to give them away?"

"I thought someone else would appreciate them," Shirley said.

"You should get something for your troubles," Newhart said. "Come upstairs and I'll give you a receipt. For taxes."

Shirley hadn't thought about taxes, but before she could object Newhart had turned and was bounding up the stairs. Shirley followed slowly, glancing up at the minister, who leaped up the stairs two at a time. He was not yet forty, she thought, and she had never seen a minister before who wore a jogging suit and tennis shoes. But then she hadn't been in church for a long time either. She'd heard talk about Newhart, heard folks in town complain that he seemed more interested in social causes than people's souls, that in the pulpit he counseled rather than preached. But then Newhart was new in town, and folks needed something to talk about, especially when the weather was constant. Shirley had long ago given up persuading Gil to go to church, not even on Christmas or Easter. She had thought about going alone, but then people would talk about her.

Newhart had disappeared into his study and Shirley was momentarily alone on the dark, narrow stairway. The wooden stairs squeaked underfoot and she remembered the feel, the texture of those steps, as she had climbed them so many times as a child in her white choir robe, an alto in the Choir of Innocents, parading up the stairs through the minister's office, out into the church to take their places in the first two pews. She had felt the eyes of the entire congregation on her then, and worried about tripping in her new Easter heels, falling on the two steps that led from the altar to the main floor and the pews.

The top of the dark stairs opened into the minister's study. Newhart had his back to her, leaning over an open desk drawer as he rummaged through papers. The room was bright, shockingly bright and colorful to Shirley, who remembered it as a dark and solemn place. A bright, blue carpet covered the old wooden floor, bookcases reached to the ceiling beside the desk where Newhart searched for a receipt. The bookcases had been stripped to a raised patina, and the spines of the books were every color imaginable. She remembered the dark varnish of the bookcases from years past and the hefty volumes that had once filled the shelves, their dark spines and gold embossed titles about grace and salvation and sin. The books were like the minister then, a large, ponderous, solemn man whose shoulders sagged beneath a large head. Often he mumbled incoherently in the pulpit, but at fiery moments he would rise to an eloquence that would stir even the deepest sleepers in the congregation. She looked at the brightly colored books with the blue, red, orange, and green spines and stark eye-catching letters. She read titles about fitness, nutrition, bonding, and lifestyle management, and then some older books, about civil rights and feminism and Vietnam, whose titles sunk into the creases of their spines. A poster of Martin Luther King hung over Newhart's desk and on an adjacent wall, a poster of one of the Kennedys. Shirley recognized the shock of hair, although she could not tell which brother it belonged to.

She heard a strain of music coming from the speaker atop the bookcase. A familiar refrain formed in her memory, but she could not place the song. Something from the car radio when she was in high school, a song she had danced to before she married Gil. She mouthed the lyrics—something's happening here—and for the first time in years she felt an urge to dance.

"How much are they worth?" Newhart asked, turning from the desk. "I"ll let you set the price."

Shirley rocked on the balls of her feet, her hips swayed slightly.

"The song's a private joke," Newhart said. "Nothing's happening here."

Shirley flushed with embarrassment. Her heels touched the floor, but the refrain still coursed through her mind.

"I don't know their value," she said. "I have no idea."

"Twenty-five? Fifty? More than that?" Newhart leaned over the desk and scribbled out a receipt. "You may as well get the money back as the government."

As Newhart wrote out the receipt, Shirley scanned the bookcases. It had just occurred to her that there was nothing in this office to indicate it was a church office. Where were the trappings of office? She searched the book titles for the mention of God.

"Do you read?" Newhart asked, holding out the receipt.

"Just some women's magazines."

Newhart swept his arms toward the books. "These are mostly for counseling. Pastoral counseling is my specialty. If people are troubled, I'll loan them a book." Then he laughed. "But as you can see, the shelves are full. Business is slow. I was warned when I came here that this is the land of silence. No one speaks."

"People don't like to bother others with their troubles," Shirley said.

"It's no bother," Newhart said.

"My troubles are no different from anyone else's."

Newhart had turned to run his fingers over the spines of the brightly colored books. How unlike the private, solemn old man who had occupied this office in her youth, Shirley thought. She could recall the vestments swaying from his neck as he lumbered to the pulpit, the mumbled sermon that seemed to exclude the congregation and encourage daydreams in a young girl; then the voice rising at unpredictable moments as he seized a point, an insight pulled from his own mumbled, private discourse, like a fish jerked from muddy water. A thought becoming a thought impelled to be heard by all. And Shirley would realize that something important had just been said, by the tone, by the sudden clear resonance of the old man's voice, but the meaning had escaped her and she would feel guilty that she had been staring at the back of Jimmy Roth's neck, entranced by the parallel lines that ran up the back of his neck before they disappeared into the soft brown line of his hair. She would feel again the eyes of the congregation on her, her sin made public; and so to assuage her guilt she would concentrate that much more on the Lord's Prayer at the end of the sermon, but even before she could form the words *on earth as it is in heaven* her thoughts would wander again, this time into a darkened closet at school, where in a game of truth-dare-double-dare she had opened her blouse to the hand of Jimmy Roth.

"You might like this," Newhart said, waving a book before her eyes.

Shirley felt the scar running across her stomach, heavy and prominent like the old man's vestments that hung from his massive shoulders. There was no pain, only the weight of the raised scar. She felt herself sagging from the shoulders, collapsing at the center.

"What's wrong?" Newhart asked, dropping the book on the desk.

"It's nothing," Shirley said. "It's all in my head."

Newhart steadied her by the arm. "You're pale," he said. "Let me help you."

Shirley shook her head in denial twice, but then felt the eyes of the congregation on her, as she had when she was a child. She flushed and righted herself and met Newhart's bewildered eyes. Impulsively she pulled up her blouse to reveal the scar.

"Look!" she cried. "Look what he did to me."

She saw Newhart's hand floating toward her stomach to touch the blemish on the smooth white skin. His fingers opened and trailed along the raised edges of that pathway, his eyes faraway in some ancient land, a garden of volcanic ruins, in a moonscape where it was hard to breathe. His fingers drifted down her stomach as Shirley remembered the parallel lines on the back of a boy's neck. She heard the mumbled liturgy and the voices in the pews behind her chorusing a response, and then the organ chord and the Choir of Innocents rising from their places and their voices swooping and parting like the swallows she had seen escaping from the loft in the barn. Her hips swayed in a motion of life that defied the eyes of the congregation. She could stare at the back of Jimmy Roth's neck during the entire service if she wanted to. If she wanted to. The thought lingered like the taste of wine coating her tongue. If she wanted to. She could stare until the parallel lines blurred and became one someplace far up into his hair, at the very tip of his skull. She could recall games of truth-dare-double-dare until the benediction and the last amen echoed from the pews behind her. If she wanted to.

Afterward, Newhart lay quietly beside her. He kissed her neck and then ran his fingers over the raised ridge of her scar.

"It feels like the fins of a fish," he said.

His hand felt heavy on her stomach; she pushed it away as if freeing herself from a fallen log.

"That's between Gil and me," she said flatly.

Newhart rolled over and reached for his clothes and dressed with his back to her. "May the Lord God bless and keep thee," he said, lacing up his running shoes and rising to his feet without turning to face her.

Shirley lay alone on the floor. A shaft of sunlight came through the high window near the bookcase, framing and warming her stomach as she lay quietly molding the memories of the day into a whole, like shaping dough into something that could be baked. The old man's heavy vestments and his darkened, solemn study, the daydreams and early longings and guilt and the swooping swallows and the Choir of Innocents; and now there was this new man, the minister, who was less real to her than the old memories, to whom no scars bound her.

It was then, lying in the study with the shaft of sunlight across her stomach, that she conceived of the dance of her own grace. A midnight dance when Gil was asleep, when his troubled snoring would echo down the hallway, and her hips would sway and her feet would stir and she could search in a rhythm of her own, in the motions of love, for the fusion of all memory and desire.

# Neither of Them Spoke, nor Wept

*It sounded first like distant rain, the answer to their prayers, then the sky turned to a brown-yellow haze that obscured the sun, and by three o'clock in the afternoon it looked like dusk.*

*In their new wood house she closed the windows, shoved towels under the doors, blankets up the chimney and then closed the door to the bedroom and her sleeping baby. As she covered the crocks of flour and corn meal and shoved the fresh bread back into the oven, the locusts descended and began pelting the roof and pinging like hard rain against the windows.*

*She pinned up her hair, glanced out the window at the rows of green corn, the ripe garden of beans and potatoes, then began whispering the Lord's Prayer as her hands wrestled with her apron. The house darkened as the locusts swarmed against the windows, and through her prayers* on earth as it is in heaven *she could hear them gnawing at the paint on the house.*

*When they chewed through the towels and blankets* thy kingdom come *she grabbed a broom and swept at the table and countertops and her new red gingham curtains. If she could only just keep them on the floor, if she could just keep them on the floor, it was all she asked, now, and then she felt them prickling against her flesh, her arms and neck and entangled in her hair, chewing. And then a flour sack burst and a white cloud floated in the air and from the safety of the bedroom the baby cried for her breast, but she didn't dare open the door.*

*Outside, her husband had built a fire and was scraping the ground with a grain shovel. The ground was alive, shifting and whirling in a yellow froth, and her husband looked like a man knee deep in a flood, trying to change its course with a stick. All that remained of his shirt was a ragged collar.*

*In two hours the locusts ascended and headed southeast; the sun and blue sky returned and a silence, deeper than they could imagine, stretched from horizon to horizon. The cornfield and garden had vanished; the chickens stumbled and reeled in stupefied bliss, the hogs were bloated, their flesh tainted beyond use, and the water in the well was putrid yellow-green.*

*That night in bed, despite the oppressive heat, they pulled a sheet and a blanket up to their shoulders. Neither of them spoke, nor wept, but between them the baby was restless and colicky and refused her breast. It tightened, coiled, then churned its legs and clenched its fists. Its breath caught in its throat, and they feared it would explode. Anything could happen now.*

# Now It Looks Respectable

There were just two of them, a man and a woman, in the little country cemetery on the day before Memorial Day, yet the distance between them was as vast as the distance between the living and the dead.

They had once been great lovers, and for a time they were married, so perhaps they had even been intimate—but that would have been a long time ago, maybe ten or twelve years ago, thought the man, whose knowledge of the past was imprecise.

His name was Vic, and this time, too, he was late to pay his respects. From the meadow where he had parked his truck he saw that Jennie was already at the grave site, her head bowed, hands folded in front—from a distance she looked like a gray statuette, a fixture among the white crosses and speckled headstones and bright wreaths, an incongruous memory in a sleepy landscape of dreams. An east wind, the kind that brings rain, lifted her dress then forced it tight against her thighs and pushed it into the crease between her legs. Then her hand rose to brush the hair from her cheek.

Vic rubbed his hands on his jeans. It was in his hands that he felt the loss. They were stained from his handyman's work and they still smelled of fish. He clenched a fist and snapped a punch into the palm of its mate, then did it again so he could feel the sting. He was afraid his hands would betray him.

He turned away and tried to spit into the rolls of sod in the back of the pickup, but his mouth was too dry. He checked again the tools he'd need for repairing the grave—the shovel and trowel and clippers—and the kerosene for cleaning the small headstone he'd sculpted himself years ago. It was from a piece of sandstone he'd found near Turk's Bluff, and on it he had inscribed "Little Fish" and the date that marked both the birth and death of the infant. The stone had left a reddish soot on his clothes and on his hands. It had stayed with him for a long time.

But today was Jennie's idea. She had found him last night at the Greener Pasture with a telephone call that had put an end to Lyle Greer's fabulous tales of an enormous, uncatchable flathead in the depths of Lake Hutanga. Vic was greeted by a business voice, a voice without attachments, a voice that seemed cool and dry and brought sandstone to mind. His fingers curled into his palms as he listened to Jennie explain that she had stopped over on her way to the coast for a meeting, to pay her respects at the cemetery, and found the grave site so ill-maintained that it was embarrassing. The grass, what little there was over the grave, was all brown and dry and so sparse that sandburrs had grown up. Something had to be done, something just had to be done, and when she demanded to know if he had even been there in all these years, Vic reached for the tape measure on his belt, pulled the tiny hook at the end of the tape and claimed he'd driven by a few times and checked it from the road. Weakened, he'd agreed to meet her the next day to repair the grave, to make it look respectable for Memorial Day.

It was kind of like a business deal, Vic thought, as he returned to the bar. The rest of the evening he leaned on the counter, absently playing with the tape measure he'd unclipped from his belt. He would uncoil it a foot or two, brood over the bizarre incongruity of intimacy and distance, then let it rattle back into its shell again. The boys in the bar, in a ritual of mock sympathy, kept buying him bottle after bottle of Coors until that incongruity dissolved into a blue-green sea of bliss.

But this morning at the M & P Cafe, Jody Hacker had leaned over as Vic was swallowing the last bite of his hash-browns and wanted to know what in Sam Hill brought his ex-wife back into town, anyhow.

"Memorial Day," Vic heard himself answer, "I guess." He fingered the tape measure on his belt and was dimly aware of some promise that had been made.

Now, at the cemetery, the sod bounced against his legs as he carried it toward the grave site. Tiny balls of the moist, dark underside broke off and rolled down his pants legs and into his boots. He was glad to hold something in his hands, ballast, as he approached the grave, as he approached Jennie.

She was hunched over, kneeling, in a posture Vic mistook for prayer. Her dark hair was like a cocoon around her face, and as he stacked the sod beside the grave he realized it wasn't prayer but writing that had brought her to her knees. On her lap was a notebook and in her hand a pen stopped then lurched across the page. He returned to the truck for the tools and caught the river scent from his hands of the carp he'd caught the day before, or perhaps it was the day before that. He'd washed his hands many times since then, but the scent lingered. In the meadow a cottontail hopped away, stopped, watched him warily, then nibbled at the tender new grass as Vic carried everything he thought that he would need to the grave.

"I pulled out the burrs while I was waiting," Jennie said, as Vic began working. She was still bowed over the notebook, but now she was biting on the end of the pen. Above her head a bee courted her hair.

An ant crawled over Vic's boot. He shook it off and started breaking the ground. He tried to be careful, gentle with the shovel, as if brushing dried skin from a wound. He outlined a rectangle, like a window frame, over the grave then skimmed off the surface to make a bed for the new sod. He roughed up the bottom to encourage a deep rooting.

"I have to get all this down," Jennie said, the pen pausing then bursting across a line. "My counselor wanted me to record everything. She said it would be cathartic and facilitate closure."

The pen surged forward, stopped, then seemed to claw at the paper, scratching its way to the bottom of the page where it stopped with a jab of punctuation. Rising from the page it became a feather stroking the cleft of her chin. She shook the hair from her face and for the first time looked at him.

"What are your feelings now, Vic?" she asked, the pen poised at the top of a new page.

Two butterflies swirled between them, landed on the broken ground, then rose and vanished on the breeze that carried them toward the meadow. Vic's hand slid up and down the handle of the shovel as his eyes followed their flight. They brought to mind a long fly ball.

"I used to play baseball over there. In that meadow," he said, nodding. "Over there! It was bigger then, like another country, and you could run forever under a fly ball. I remember how white the ball was against the blue sky, kinda like the belly of a fish.

"On Memorial Day, after the salute and gunfire and "Faith of Our Fathers" a bunch of us kids would get up a game using pie tins or broken branches for bases. One time, I don't remember for sure who it was, but it must have been Allen whatever his name was, that husky kid with the freckled face and big round chest. He must have been an orphan or something—he just stayed around here for a year or two with his aunt and uncle—but I remember that one day he hit one way over my head out in center field. Jesus, it was like a shooting star.

"I remember trying to look at the sky and the ground at the same time, trying to watch the ball against the blue sky and watch my feet so I didn't trip over any crosses or markers—that's how far he hit it—way out of the meadow into the cemetery!

"I ran as hard as I could, jumping over graves and flowers but it came down behind me anyway and started rolling and ricocheting off headstones like a pinball; but then all of a sudden it ricocheted right to me. I'll be damned! It caromed right to me. Right in my glove. In my hands!" He paused, staring out into the meadow where the butterflies had disappeared; a child's delight shone on his face.

"Without even looking I wheeled and threw home, and as soon as I let go with the throw I caught sight of home plate, how far away it was, just a speck in the horizon, just a tiny speck, but something happened—I don't know what, but somehow the ball rose and rose and soared and soared just like a dream and the next thing I knew it smacked into Michael Ludvik's glove and he slapped a tag across Big Al's ankle just as slick as anything you'd ever see on television."

He was leaning on the shovel, his hands folded over the end of the handle, grinning. He was so happy. But when he glanced at Jennie he suddenly felt foolish, unsure of what he was saying or why he was saying it. He'd gotten carried away and revealed too much.

But she had put the notebook aside and was digging at the ground with the pen, as if chipping ice. Grains of sand flew up and stuck to her dark hose. She pulled the hem of her skirt down to her knees.

"I wanted to bring some wildflower seeds," she said softly, eying the grave. "Lots of wildflower seeds. Black-eyed Susans and bachelor buttons and sunflowers and poppies and cosmos . . . all my favorite wildflowers. I even dreamed once about wildflowers spreading from here and taking over the cemetery. They were so pretty, swaying in the breeze." She stared at the ground she'd disturbed with the pen, then began smoothing it, patting it down.

"But the cemetery isn't a place for wild things," she said, abruptly rising to her feet and brushing the dried grass from her skirt.

The floss of dandelions drifted in the breeze and clung to her hair like snow. The scent of rain vanished and the small, marbled clouds fled into the west. In the northern hills a silent hawk rose above Turk's Bluff and in the dark corridor of trees that lined the river to the south some desperate crows squawked and chattered.

Viewed from above the cemetery was a serene refuge, the hub of order within the surrounding fields and the grid of gravel roads.

On opposite ends of the grave they each went to work. While Vic rolled out the sod Jennie cleaned the stone. It was coated with dust from the fields and speckled with droppings from the many birds that had used it for a perch while hunting insects in the grass. Clumps of abandoned spiderwebs were matted against the stone like wet hair. Jennie picked off the webs then cleaned each letter and number on the stone as if wiping sleep from the crusted corner of a child's eye.

The name "Little Fish" had come from Vic, because that's how the stillborn infant had appeared to him at the time; and Jennie, too embittered at the time to dignify death with a proper name from life, had acquiesced. But that had been a long time ago, and recently, as a way of easing herself into sleep, she'd lay in bed and let her mind wander through all the proper names she could think of . . . all the Justins and Matthews and Austins and Jonahs . . . never settling on one before falling asleep, but for some reason the possibilities soothed her, allowed her to slip into a comfortable sleep.

During that first year she had been wild with a grief that had turned into an arrogant, reckless defiance. Then, in the death throes of their marriage, she and Vic had fought and loved with a terminal passion.

It culminated here on the grave, on what would have been the child's first birthday; after a night of dancing she was defiantly happy and determined that they should bring a bottle of wine and some bread to the cemetery to celebrate a life that never was. There was bitter salvation in the irony—and the sharpest of it would make her laugh and snap her head and send her hair lashing through the air.

It was one of those spring nights when the moon was hazy and there was a sultry charge in the wind that made her feel crazy and vile and immune from misfortune because it was misfortune that sustained her. She'd hugged the bottle of red wine and Vic palmed the bread as they wandered back and forth through the cemetery under the dull light of the moon, offering toasts and a chorus of "This Little Light of Mine" to the names they found inscribed along the way.

When they finally reached their son's grave they pitched the blanket and planted a lighted match in the ground. Jennie was quick to blow it out before it could burn out; she laughed, clapped her hands, then took a drink and sang "Happy Birthday" before rising to her feet and taking the first steps of an improvised dance. She swirled like a leaf caught in an eddy, her arms spread to encircle a huge imaginary partner, and her head tilted back to face a sky full of whirling stars. The wine splashed from the bottle in her hand, trickled down a bare leg, stained her bare feet and dried in the grass. It splashed on Vic, who rose and tried to dance with her but surrendered when he realized that her spirit for dance was so much larger than his.

When she collapsed next to him on the blanket, they passed the wine and bread back and forth, swaying and bumping shoulders, bouncing off one another as Jennie began singing silly children's songs. Her hands illustrated the songs, carved images in the air to accompany "Itsy Bitsy Spider" and "It's a Small World" and then again "This Little Light of Mine"—the whole time laughing and rocking back and forth, a part of her still dancing because she was so happy because it was working so magnificently—the song and the drink and the dancing and the sultry wind and the irreverence subduing all those crazy daytime feelings that whirled around in her stomach like wild, wounded birds.

It was still working when she lay back and felt Vic's tongue licking the wine that was drying on her thigh; she was still dancing, still singing, still creating images in the air with her hands even as she slid out of her clothes. When he filled the space above her, her hands stopped against his chest, explored it like a darkened wall, then slapped at it as if killing a spider, laughed, then pulled him closer, down to her, and bit at his neck.

For a moment, hovering over her, pinning her arms, he eclipsed the moon and shielded her from the warm wind; she couldn't breathe the way she wanted so she struggled free and pushed him away, but then some old fear, some darkness interceded and she despised both his absence and his presence, and then she despised the damp ground that had first felt so good against her hips and the thick sultry air that was so exhilarating—she despised it, its heaviness, its weight—and when she arched her back and pushed up against him, she didn't know if she was resisting him or some infliction in the air. She raked her nails at whatever was in front of her, drew blood from his cheek, cried out, and then pulled him down to her, clung to him and felt so relieved to finally lash out against some flesh and blood other than her own. She felt something warm, wine or blood, on her breasts, and when she rolled free she started shaking uncontrollably; her lips quivered, her hands shook until she hugged herself and coiled up in the blanket with her back to Vic and the headstone, and finally was able to sob quietly into the darkness.

Vic lay a hand on the blanket, on her hip, as if steadying a rattle, and looked up at the stars because he didn't know what to say. A thin streak of blood stained his cheek.

Now, twelve years later, he was on his hands and knees, pressing down the sod, trying to make everything just right. The edges had to be flush, and the seams fused, so it would look nice for Memorial Day. Rising to his feet he methodically walked toe-to-heel over the seams, using his weight to fuse the separate pieces. When he stepped back to look he wasn't sure that it was better than before. The rich grass, the neat rectangle, the clean stone—for some reason it all made him afraid. He looked at Jennie, started to say something but cleared his throat instead; the hand that had begun to reach across the grave stopped in midair and retreated to the tape measure on his belt.

The day was moving on and the breeze had stopped. It was that time of the afternoon when the birds were silent. The caretaker, an old man in coveralls, circled the meadow on a riding mower.

Other people had come into the cemetery and were arranging flowers or stooping to pull dandelions from graves. An older couple who wore matching glasses made their way around the graves, pausing to point at the headstone or comment on a family name. She carried a wreath and he carried a tripod, and as they wandered from grave to grave, the distance between them always remained the same.

Jennie took the tiny wreath from the florist's sack and lay it carefully beside the clean headstone. The red flowers were bright against the fresh green sod.

"There," she said, rising, "now it looks respectable."

## Touched by the Warm Life

*In the hills to the north, beyond Turk's Bluff, there was a chief, a brilliant tyrant, who, in revenge against the Ponca's raid, murdered their two peacemakers carrying pipes. But when the beautiful daughter of the Ponca chief was sent out, he accepted her, adored her, married her, sired three children, and then one night in a whiskey rage slashed her throat with his hunting knife.*

*For seventeen days afterward he sat on the bank of the Quivira River and mourned her with a buffalo robe shrouding his head. He was near death when a tribesman brought his youngest child to him and placed the chief's cold foot on the child's neck. Touched by the warm life again under his foot, he rose, took up his duties, and went on to lead his people in their last raids, their last hunts, their final dances.*

*When he died of smallpox, so the story goes, he was buried on a standing horse beside the Quivira River.*

# Dust Devils

So we stood over the grave and drank for Will-Jonah, older than anyone's memory, and argued over where he came from.

Some said he was an Indian, others that he was a Viking. Some said that he had sired himself in some distant dawn before history, that somehow, out of that primordial muck, in a chemical reaction that only a scientist or maybe an old mule would understand, Will-Jonah had been deposited on shore—standing there with a day's growth of beard, the soiled shirt and khaki pants stained green from alfalfa and sweat, taking off the crumpled Stetson and waving it toward the valley below, cursing: "It's the raspberry shits."

There were no stories to tell about his youth or his middle age, only about his old age and his death, as if he had always been old and had always lived here in the rocky hills above the valley, on the only spot of native grass that remained in the country. He worked there, broke horses there, and worked among the weathered outbuildings on the ground patterned with gullies, the soft sandstone washing out through the years like the old man's wrinkled face.

There was a time when he lived unnoticed, but when all the old frame houses began coming down and the ranch houses went up and the gravel driveways marked a house accessible to your neighbors, Will-Jonah's front yard of tall prairie grass and long-rutted, twisting driveway caused people to talk.

Still, everyone knew that if you had a problem with a horse, Will-Jonah was the man to see. Those who remembered would tell you that the draft horses he trained could pull a plow through the toughest gumbo ground, and his saddle horses—there was no question about it—you could just give them their heads.

I

Will-Jonah leaned against the weathered barn board, pissing into the wind. The narrow channel of his piss cut its way through the dust, circling past a clump of buffalo grass then around a piece of sandstone before finally damming up and drying out against a rotting horse collar in the dry weeds. If he drank enough, he thought, he could piss a flood that would forge channels the size of rivers running down the hillside to the valley and town below. A tumbleweed, bleached bone white, blew against his leg as he zipped up. Will-Jonah kicked it away and walked back inside the barn.

He sat on the hard-dirt floor, his back against a bale of hay at the end of the stall. The stall was empty, and had been for a very long time; its last occupant, Flora, still had her name scrawled above the manger. There were names above the other stalls, too, carved years ago into the splintered oak beams. Some of the names had been crossed out, like days on the calendar, and other names written over them. There was no name and no stall for the gelding that lay dead out in the pasture. The gelding had been left with him (to break of some bad habit he could no longer remember) and had never been picked up. He had called the horse a son of a bitch and had let it have the run of the barn.

Once before Will-Jonah had leaned against a bale of hay in the same spot, drinking Ancient Age. He had forgotten that Flora was next to him and flipped an empty bottle of whiskey into the stall. The bottle bounded off Flora's rump. The mare kicked at the falling bottle, catching Will-Jonah flush on the right ankle. Her hoof shattered his ankle, though he did not know it until he sobered up three days later. He realized then that if he had never sobered up, he would never had known the pain.

Pain for him now was like the fine dust on the hillside, a part of the terrain. For days, maybe for weeks or even months, he would not notice it was there; then it would whip up behind a strong wind, dust devils that would bore right through him, swirling around in his stomach for days on end. He drank the whiskey then to settle the dust, and he always drank it here, in the barn that was more his home than the house fifty yards away. He would drink until the blue-green waves swelled up, sweeping in over the dust, leaving him weak and sometimes queasy. Then he would lie down and sleep, sometimes for days, and awake finally a new man, flushed clean for a while of the old life.

This morning he had awakened with the dust swirling in his stomach; he lay on his back for a long time, not wanting to sleep and not wanting to get up either, until he saw the first bars of light coming through the bedroom blinds. He walked to the kitchen and started the coffee, then pulled on his pants and made his way out through the door, across the rocky yard and around back to the barn. He walked through the dying milkweed to the spot where the gelding had beaten down the tall weeds to get at the sparse grass; there he saw it, its nose flat against the ground, its legs stiff and stretched out from its body. He walked up to the gelding and stood silently over it for a moment; then he kicked a blanket of dust up over its head.

He returned to the house and finished making the coffee. He sat at the kitchen table, stared at the pump next to the sink and watched the water drip from the spout down to the growing rust stain below, slowly drinking his coffee. He tucked a pinch of snooze into his cheek, tasted the coffee running over it, and recalled in meticulous detail every wrong he had ever been subjected to.

It was midmorning when he took the bottle down from the shelf next to the sink. He did not uncap it then but walked outside, across the yard to the barn, where he stood in the doorway looking out over the rocky pasture, where the dead gelding lay hidden from view by the tall weeds in the corral. He hoisted the bottle in salute and took the first swallow.

Across the pasture to the south, where the ground sloped gradually down into the valley, he saw the dust kicking up a cloud beyond the fence line. The small speck of a tractor came into view as it made the turn at the end of the field. It was Farley planting wheat. The ground was not good for wheat, and Will-Jonah had told Farley, years ago when he first plowed up the grassland, that wheat there would never yield worth a damn. But Farley was a farmer and had no use for grassland; every year he worked the ground for a small yield. In the summer of drought years the fine dust from Farley's field would blow into enormous clouds, covering everything Will-Jonah owned.

Sometimes Farley, when he was drunk, would stop by and share a bottle with Will-Jonah, complaining the whole time about the government or the low price of wheat or the high price of fuel and equipment. Will-Jonah's complaints were not in any of those categories, so he seldom had much to say to Farley, but he listened a lot and sometimes remembered when men would complain about the weather or about the grasshoppers or worry about blight taking over their fields. It occurred to Will-Jonah that the complaints of other men had changed while his had remained the same. The dust devils swirling in Farley's stomach were different from the ones swirling in his; a jump in the market could settle the dust for Farley. Will-Jonah yearned for something else.

Now the shaft of sunlight in the doorway of the barn warmed him as only the fall sunlight could. The air this time of year was clean, the sunlight unfiltered and warm. If a man was smart, he soaked up as much of the autumn sun as he could, the way you were smart to start putting up firewood. Out in the open, though, it was cool, and he did not worry about the dead gelding. By tomorrow morning the coyotes and buzzards would feel lucky and ready for winter, too.

The frame of sunlight in the doorway drew up tighter, finally creeping back outside as the sun moved behind the overhang of the roof. Will-Jonah walked away from the door, back inside toward the bale of hay at the end of Flora's stall. He slouched against the bale and drank from the bottle; his knees forked out like a woman awaiting her lover. He thought of Aggie, who would come to him at night when her husband was gone. Yesterday? Or forty years ago? His chin sagged against his chest. His eyes were on the old boots, the leather cracked and weathered so that he thought he was looking into a mirror. The cuffs of his pants, rolled to the instep of the boots, were full of hayseeds and stems. It was Will-Jonah's joke that during hard times he could empty his cuffs and plant forty acres of alfalfa. And God knows, there might be a pint or two in there, as well; a man never knew.

He finished the whiskey and threw the empty bottle into the stall. It banged against the wall and landed in the pile of empty bottles that had collected there through the years of dust devils.

He left the barn and made his way across the yard to the lone hedge tree near the house. The tree was twisted and gnarled after years of exposure and strong wind. One long branch arched out almost parallel to the ground, and under the branch was parked the GMC pickup, Will-Jonah's single concession to modern life. The Jimmy was old but it ran well, Will-Jonah claimed, because every day he poured oats into the gas tank.

The door was sprung and the harsh friction of steel against steel made Will-Jonah shiver as he popped open the door. The torn seat cover, the stuffing, and the springs in the seat had all yielded to habit and form and gently cradled the old man's rump.

The truck shook and rattled down the eroded driveway, past the rolling hills of grass and Farley's dusty fields to the blacktop a quarter of a mile away. Will-Jonah stopped when he reached the blacktop and rolled up the window. The window was cracked and held together with a pattern of tape. The alignment was off too; so to roll it up, Will-Jonah had to hold it level with one hand and crank it with the other. He would leave the window down all summer; then roll it up each fall when the first frost was just around the corner.

Each year, it seemed, the window had to be rolled up earlier and each year more wind blew through the top and bottom, whistling in through the taped cracks.

II

In Paradise there was the Greener Pasture, the only bar in town, and Will-Jonah didn't much care for it. But then life didn't always leave you with choices, which was probably a better deal anyway, he figured, since it lessened worry and probably saved a man from making the wrong choice as usual.

Bars were like anthills full of lies, and any man worth his salt would drink alone, face things square up, he figured.

His intention was to have a couple of drinks and then buy a bottle to take home, and if anyone asked him about the horse business, pried into his affairs, he would just tell them that he was plumb out of the business, that his last one had just passed on to that golden field of oats in the sky.

So he sat alone at the bar, on a stool patched together with duct tape, staring up at the wall that looked like it'd been bricked in, layer upon layer, with fancy bottles.

Marge, keeper of a small town's secret life, was washing glasses in a sinkful of soapy water, rinsing and stacking them on a rack. A bubble of soap caught in her hair. When she turned from the sink and wiped the bar, Will-Jonah leaned back and let his arms fall to his lap.

"Looks clean enough to me," he said.

"What'll it be, hon?" she asked.

"A beer and a bump would do the job. Ancient Age. I got to get ready for winter. A man needs his antifreeze."

Marge smiled. "You bet. That's what we're here for. To keep folks thawed out."

"Hey, sweetheart, we're dry over here," yelled a voice from a table beside the jukebox.

"Hold your horses," Marge yelled back. "And I ain't been nobody's sweetheart in ten years or more. And I'm sure as hell not yours."

When the door creaked open Marge looked up. "Well, mercy be," she said. "Someone in here must have a note due."

W. C. "Ike" Bryant, the banker, nodded and touched the brim of his hat, acknowledging everyone in the bar before pulling up a stool next to Will-Jonah.

"Business or pleasure, your honor," Marge said.

Bryant took off his hat and set it on the bar. "Hell, it's all business, Marge. You know that. It's what makes the world go around."

In his glass office at the bank Bryant could usually be seen with his shiny black boots up on the desktop and a sheaf of paper in his hands as a customer fidgeted in his chair, awaiting a decision on a loan. More than anything else in life Bryant loved that moment between request and approval or rejection of a loan—usually a farmer cleaned up for the day, dressed in his goin'-to-town clothes, edged forward on his chair while Bryant stretched out the moment like a rubber band. Then he would gaze at the portrait of Eisenhower on the wall, reminisce about the true greatness of the Republic after the war—loaning money at four percent, admiring the new houses going up and all the new cars and refrigerators and the children conceived in the midst of plenty. Sometimes his voice would choke or he would fall into a deep nostalgia that left him melancholy or morose.

Marge filled his glass with ice and Johnny Walker.

"That's what Ike drank," Bryant said. "At Normandy, the night before the invasion."

"Yes sir," he said then, turning to Will-Jonah, "you're just the man I want to see."

"I'm out of the horse business. Last one just died on me."

Bryant loosened the bolo tie from around his neck and unbuttoned his shirt collar. When he leaned toward Will-Jonah he spoke softly out of the corner of his mouth, as if sharing a tip on the market.

"I've got this mare and she's havin' a son of a bitch of a time foalin' " he said. "I got a hell of a lot tied up in her and I'd just hate like hell to lose her."

He winked at Marge as she carried a beer to the table beside the jukebox. "I got her as part of a foreclosure deal out west. She's a real classy mare and worth a pretty penny or two."

The banker listed the mare's bloodlines and the tax advantages of keeping livestock around. Will-Jonah wondered what the hell the world was coming too. He had another drink, but it only fed his contempt for what he called "paper horses," and when a fresh bottle of Ancient Age appeared he protested. "I'm out of the business."

But Bryant pulled a wad of bills from a thick wallet with "Ike" stamped on the front. Will-Jonah eyed the bills, calculating how much antifreeze they would buy. Enough to keep thawed out till Thanksgiving anyway, he figured.

In the banker's El Dorado they followed Main Street where it curved out of town and became a state highway, running straight and flat past the brown fields of newly seeded wheat and stubbled fields of cornstalks. Bryant found the markets on the radio and tapped his fingers on the steering wheel with each report. Will-Jonah shifted his weight on the hard vinyl seat and longed for the comfort of a hay bale, the fertile scent of his barn.

"I don't use them a helluva lot," Bryant was saying. "But it don't hurt to keep 'em around. The grandkids like to ride 'em, and it kinda helps a man keep in touch with the way things used to be."

Glancing out the window he waved his hand in the direction of a field of fallow ground.

"Hell, I had a chance to buy that section last year and like a damn fool I didn't. I just had too much tied up in other things at the time. Just didn't have the liquidity. Don't let this get around but I got good reason to believe there's a few barrels of oil under that ground."

Will-Jonah uncapped the bottle, sipped and passed it to Bryant.

"If we got to pull her I'll need a rope and some antiseptic," he said.

"If I don't have it I can get it," Bryant said. "Hell, I was goin' to call Doc but the son of a bitch charges an arm and a leg. Hell, with the cost of doctorin' it hardly pays to stay alive."

From the blacktop they followed the gravel road to a driveway that ran between white rail fences. A sign over the driveway read "Ike's Quarter Horses." They drove under the sign, up the driveway toward the white-columned house, then circled around to the barn in back. The barn was a bright red with white trim windows, and over the large double doors in front stretched a replica of the sign over the driveway.

Bryant drove through the corral gate alongside the barn then stopped at the large open door in back.

He motioned toward the dark interior of the barn.

"She's in there—laboring pretty hard. Hell, I don't know if what she's doin' is natural or not."

From inside the car Will-Jonah looked out across the pasture that stretched east as far as he could see. It swept down toward a gully that sliced the pasture in half; the tall grass rose to a patch of timber on a hill, lush and green and darkening with the fading light. It was like the pasture Aggie would cross at night when she came to him. But there was the fence she had to cross, a barbwire fence, which caught her dress.

"In here," Bryant said, leading the way through a thicket of buzzing flies seeking the last light of the day.

In the corner of the barn the mare raised her head, whinnied, then sagged back to the straw floor. Her sides heaved with her hard panting. As Bryant and Will-Jonah passed the bottle the old man listened, as if inside that hollow breath was an answer to a mystery.

"How long she been working at it?"

"Long enough," Bryant said, taking the bottle. "The missus called me at the office this morning. But I was tied up for awhile and couldn't get away."

Beneath the slotted manger filled with hay, the mare lifted her head at Will-Jonah's approach, then lay her head back down when he knelt beside her and stroked her under the mouth.

"It's a son of a bitch, old girl. A real son of a bitch, ain't it." He kept his hand on her flesh, trailing his fingers over her back as he moved behind her. He stroked her rump a few times, then slid his hand down to her dilated opening. Two hooves protruded.

"That's $20,000 worth of horseflesh," Bryant said. "She's a beauty, ain't she?"

The mare lifted her head, then jerked it high in the air. She rolled forward as she tried for the momentum to swing herself up, but soon she settled down, breathing hard from the effort.

"You think we'll have to pull her?"

"She needs help," Will-Jonah said, taking a rope down from a peg and squatting next to the mare. He pulled the loop tight around the two protruding hooves then took up the slack as he braced himself with one foot on the ground and the other on the mare's haunches.

"Okay, girl. You just take it easy now. We'll do the work for you." When he leaned back on the rope, the mare's rump jerked into the air and her nose dipped into the straw, spraying up clouds of straw and dust.

Again he pulled, and again, until he was breathing hard, panting in rhythm with the laboring mare. Her eyes were wild with a confused terror—the thwarted instinct for flight more terrifying than the labor itself, as Will-Jonah, alone, leaned back on the rope until his hands slipped, the rope slackened, and he slumped to his knees behind the mare.

"Christ," he panted.

"Maybe it's a breech of some kind," Bryant said. "We could get Doc out here."

Will-Jonah rolled back from his knees and leaned against the side of the barn. The rope, still tied to the two small hooves, trailed across his lap.

"I'll go call Doc," Bryant said.

"Where's the bottle?" Will-Jonah searched his back pocket, then felt through the straw.

"I got it," Bryant said.

Will-Jonah sipped from the bottle until his breathing slowed. "We don't need any goddamned vet," he said.

He didn't realize how dark it had gotten until Bryant flipped a light switch. The sky beyond the doorway was changing to fiery colors of purple-crimson, darkening slowly around the edges as the sun slipped west, over the barn, leaving a dark slate behind.

After his last swallow he flipped the bottle into the far corner of the barn, where it thumped into the straw. Standing up, he staggered then steadied himself against a stall before taking a step toward the mare.

"Doc could be out here in fifteen minutes," Bryant said.

"We can ease her out with your car," Will-Jonah said, leaning over the mare, stroking her as she lay quietly resting between the heaves of storm.

Bryant had the feeling of riding a losing market as he backed up the car to the barn door. Will-Jonah checked the rope around the small hooves then let it trail through his fingers like a guide as he made his way to the bright red taillights and the rising cloud of exhaust thinning out into the night air.

"I could call Doc," Bryant said. "That's $20,000 worth of horse."

Will-Jonah crawled under the bumper of the El Dorado, hitched the rope to an angled brace. "You comfort your mare," he told Bryant. "I'll just ease it up a little."

He felt his way along the car until he reached the front door. Inside, his hardened hands wrapped around the padded steering wheel. A window buzzed shut when his elbow grazed a button on the door. Everything he touched was of another world. The array of lights stretching across the panel looked like fireflies on a vine. His foot found the accelerator, but even then he couldn't hear the engine, nor could he hear the tortured panting of the laboring mare.

In the mirror, in the barn light, he could see Bryant's eyes, more terrified than the mare's.

"She's getting restless," he shouted.

Will-Jonah shifted into low drive and idled forward to take up the slack. He felt tired and his eyes burned. He blinked and stared straight ahead, his field of vision smaller than the wedge of light carved by the headlights.

Within that wedge was an eerie stillness like the silence before a storm—when a good one was coming, and God was stingy with the air, and the lungs ached just trying to survive, not even prosper, just survive—and then the water would come, not as rain from the sky but in blue-green waves from the horizon, thick and heavy enough to press his ancient bones into fossils. He could feel the change, a wet poison seeping into his skin in advance of the flood.

Under his foot the accelerator flattened, and the tires spun, forging a wall of dust as Bryant heard the engine roar and watched his El Dorado vanish into the dust and darkness. The rope cracked like a whip, then the mare bellowed and her hooves scrabbled as she tried to brace herself on the floor sliding beneath her.

Bryant fell back against the wall as his eyes swung from the mare to the roar in the darkness, the dull taillights moving away out into the night.

Then a wet rending noise like the slap of water filled the barn as the mare and foal were torn asunder. Her haunches sagged into a viscous pool of blood, freed finally from her foal, freed finally from life itself.

It was several minutes before a confused Bryant left the light of the barn and made his way through the darkness of the pasture, down to the gully, to the wreckage of his El Dorado and the body of the foal. Feeling his way along the ground he found the foal, brushed the thistles and dirt from its wet flesh and then, as his eyes dilated, he saw that the rope that had dragged the foal stillborn into the world was wrapped around a front and a rear hoof.

We buried them on the hillside overlooking the valley to the north, on high ground where the digging was hard, and we had to use a pick more than a shovel. It took five of us all day to dig the three graves, but by sunset we had finished and lowered the bones of the gelding first, then the foal, and finally we lowered Will-Jonah into the ground. We would have buried the mare, too, but Bryant had her rendered out for fifty bucks.

Farley produced the pint of Ancient Age, and we each took a shot; then he recapped it and threw it into the grave with the old man. The bottle landed in the dry earth at the bottom of the hole next to Will-Jonah's hand.

*The whiskey, Farley said, would help settle the dust.*

# The Wonder of His Levitation

*Ol' Cinch, the bachelor, had come in early from the fields because of the menace of the storm, the low, dark slab like an oiled whetstone sliding across the sky, the quick burst of lightning flicking like a snake's tongue from the darkness.*

A good one is coming, that's for sure, *he thought, but he was a man who'd survived two floods, a fire, been knocked from a haystack by lightning, yielded three fingers on his right hand to a combine sickle, sacrificed a lung to friendly fire in Korea, and once spent a night in a blizzard hunkered down against a dead Angus cow.*

*As he pushed his sock down over his heel and picked at the thistles in the mesh, he glanced out of the kitchen window, past the sinkful of dishes, and saw the charcoal funnel spinning down from the belly of the dark cloud. It looked like the naked leg of a dancer as it toed the ground north of the river then bent and spun across the straight rows of new corn, and for a moment he was mesmerized by its fierce beauty.*

*There was a roar, fierce as the surf, then a rattle, like loose bearings. Cinch shook out his boots, but before he had time to stuff his socks into his boots the floor vanished in a crackling explosion, and he was plunged into a tunnel of darkness then lifted into a swirling blue-pink cloud, a dream, clutching his socks, while around him whirled pots and pans and dishes, shingles and splintered boards—the hood of his Chevy truck sailed past and a box of oatmeal, and he remembered his socks in his hands, and it seemed terribly important at that moment to find his boots and finish what he had begun but he couldn't move his hand nor could he tell what was up or what was down. The debris of his life whirled around him as he spun inside the dream with leaden hands.*

*Then, as abruptly as he had ascended, he fell, jolted like a child falling from bed, and he beheld a deep blue sky holding fast above him as the vapor of a jet, like gray sutures, rose into space.*

*He arched his neck, wiggled his toes, and reclaimed his breath. A cool moisture oozed through his shirt and a familiar odor—a stench that had always been downwind—came to him and in place of the blue sky he was looking up into the face of a Yorkshire sow, its ears drooping over its eyes like half-drawn shades and its snout five inches from his face. It grunted, turned away, and began rooting at a phone book in the wallow. Only then did he realize that he has been transported a half mile away, to his neighbor's place.*

*As he slowly stood up and began picking the splinters from his flesh, it occurred to him that it had been years since he'd kept hogs. Maybe it was something a guy ought to get back into. The market was pretty good. And he had enough feed. He scraped the muck from his arms and backside, reeled until he got his bearings, stepped over the low fence and followed the trail of debris across a wheat field back to his home. Along the way he picked up a glove and some underwear and a can of pork 'n' beans. In the midst of the rubble, where the kitchen had been, he found his boots, exactly where he'd left them. It was hard to figure, he thought, as he shoved the socks into the boots.*

*In late June, when the neighbors helped him rebuild, they compared the tornado to worse ones they'd known. They shook their heads over the price of flooring and shingles and complained about the bindweed in a neighbor's field. Ol' Cinch never spoke of the wonder of his levitation, his journey through the heavens, flying like an angel, except once at the Greener Pasture, after too much to drink, and then he lied and changed the ending to a field of clover; but even then he was kindly ridiculed, and told if it was all true, it was as close to heaven as he would get.*

# A Free Sinner

"He was as high-headed a son of a bitch as I ever seen. High-headed as hell. Hell, a man would just sneak a look in the direction of the corral and those ears would shoot up like an ol' boy's pecker. And that ol' head would go up, and he'd snort and then take off just lickety-split like there was no tomorrow by God, and, hell, that was even before that rodeo contractor and that Gloria gal stuck their noses into it.

"Hell, I don't know why they didn't just shoot 'im in the very beginning. That's what I would-a done. Saved a lot of grief and commotion, but you know how folks get when they're contestin' somethin'."

Leo was shaking his head. "It was the goddamnedest thing. The goddamnedest farm auction I ever been to. A circus, I tell ya. A regular circus." He tongued the chaw in his cheek up a little higher, pushed it up into his gums, worked it around for a while, then leaned to the side and spit into an empty Coors can.

There must have been a half dozen of the boys sitting around the table at the Greener Pasture, listening, mostly, to Leo, although some of the boys came and went, drifted off to shoot a game of pool or claimed the missus wanted him home. It must have been close to eleven o'clock, and the dance floor was empty except for that heavy-set gal from out of town and that little, wiry parts salesman who always acted like he was trying to crawl inside her as they swayed back and forth like a couple of weeds all tangled up in the wind. So it must have been Monday night. Before football season.

"What'd the 6–10 bring?" Farley asked.

"Hell, I don't think it brung two," Leo said.

"Three and a quarter," a voice said. It was Carl. He was good with figures. He'd clerked the sale, and he was drinking coffee.

"It'd been sitting idle for a long time. Out there in the granary."

"It couldn't a had too many hours on it."

"It had a few, I guess."

"Front-end loader sold it," Carl said, as he stacked Leo's loose change on the table.

"Hell, I was too busy chasin' that goddamned horse around to remember," Leo said. He leaned back on the legs of his chair and balanced himself with a boot on the edge of the table. His straw hat, stained by sweat around the band, was perched on the back of his head, above the white line of his forehead, and when he laughed, his belly would jostle his bottle of Coors and a little foam would ooze onto his lap.

"I never seen nothin' like it. Never. It was a circus. A goddamned circus, I tell ya."

"It commenced right on time, 11:00," Carl said.

"I heard it was a pretty fair turnout for August, considering how humid it was."

"Could-a been worse."

"Made enough to cover the widow's costs at the home."

"I tell ya, word sure can get out and travel nowadays, and not just when you don't want it to neither."

"They even got rid of those ol' toothless roan cows?"

"B & T Packing," Carl said. "McDonalds."

"Everthing was purty regular," Leo said, "till long about 4–5 o'clock (*3:30,* Carl said), and the boys that was left crowded around the corral, and the Colonel he got his second wind and swung into high gear and climbed up on the fence and started in with that megaphone like he was offering up quarter sections of the promised land, cheap."

*Boys,* he said, *boys, now gather up boys,* he said. *We got a deal for you. We got what you been waitin' for. You betcha. For the money this is as fine a horse as you ever goin't get.*

"And I'll be damned if he didn't start recitin' a pedigree that sounded like one of those Old Testament deals and even went so far as to claim its name was Sinner, and I knew for a fact right then and there he was a storyin' just to build up interest.

"Hell, by the time he got through talkin' that horse up, you would-a thought it could-a pulled a plow in the mornin', ran for the roses in the afternoon, and still have enough spunk left over to rope in the national Finals and service forty-five rank mares all in the same day, I tell ya.

"Hell, truth was he was as gaunt a saddle sore and foundered and snake-mean a son of a bitch as I ever seen. And the minute the Colonel started braggin' 'im up, that ol' head shot up, those ears got a hard-on, and he went crazy. Just plumb loco, out-of-this-world crazy. Like he wanted nothin' to do with being bought and sold.

"Hell, he started rearin' and buckin' and spinnin', and those godawful white eyes blared like a couple of head-lights and before you knowd it, he'd took that fence like nothin' and sent folks scramblin' over each another like a funnel sightin'. Made a man think, momentarily at least, that maybe all that braggin' was the Gospel truth.

"Then I saw that rodeo man, that contractor, hangin' back like he had been the whole sale, leanin' on that tractor tire with his boot up against the tread, still working that toothpick, with that hat pulled low against the sun so you couldn't even tell if he had eyes or not. He didn't so much as twitch when that wild son of a bitch shot by 'im. Hell, he looked like he was appraisin' it."

"He must a been a Texan," someone said.

"He was a cool cucumber," Leo said. "He just hung back the whole sale, workin' that toothpick under the shade of that big ol' Stetson like he owned the world. Hell, that big ol' silver buckle he had reflected more sunlight than any galvanized roof I ever seen."

"Plated silver," Carl said.

"Hell, whatever it was, it sure was bright. Anyway, he sure seemed pleased with what he seen when ol' Sinner tore past him. He just nodded and didn't move a muscle the whole time that high-headed son of a bitch tore around the yard and started jumpin' plumb over racks and scatterin' folks right and left and rearin' just like Trigger used to on TV. Hell, it was kind of purty, if you ask me, just like one of those hood ornaments on one of those ol' Pontiacs."

"Mustangs," Carl said.

"Never owned one," Leo said, "but by God that son of a bitch sure enough looked like he'd come back from the dead. Hell, resurrected. A Jesus horse!"

"Had he ever been bucked out?" Farley asked.

"Not in this lifetime," Leo said.

"Some of the boys found an ol' kinked-up rope on one of the racks, but they could no more rope a fence post than spit, and they ended up getting' all tangled up and floppin' around like a bunch of minnows in a bucket of spit until I thought we was goin' to have an accidental hangin' before the day was through.

"Doc, he was there, buyin' that ol' harness for the missus to use as a decoration in that new house he's buildin' (*a quarter million,* Carl said, *at least*), and he goes to his truck and gets out that tranquilizer gun he uses on rank bulls and rabid dogs, and in all the commotion and shoutin', ol' Sinner spooked again just when they had 'im cornered, and the dart just whizzed on by, and wouldn't you know it, caught ol' Elmer across the yard aways just as he was bendin' over to pick up that rockin' chair he bought for a quarter. (*Dime, I believe,* Carl said.)

"Rump shot 'im, by God. Right in the ass, and it wasn't five minutes before he was curled up on that stack a warped two by fours just a sleepin' like a baby. Hell, I guess the missus she came on him like that and just started in on 'im about sleepin' his life away as usual and havin' no more shame than doin' it in public like this, but ol' Elmer, I guess, even when he came to, never got too riled up—he just smiled at her and walked around with that dart stickin' in his ass. Wouldn't let Doc pull it neither, said it would bust up his marriage.

"I guess he went to church on Sunday and spent the whole service standin' up in a corner. Slept like a mule."

"Ol' Sinner got free?" Farley asked.

"It looked like a clean break. He had clear sailin' down the road, but then ol' Lyle (*Gil,* Carl said) who was just leavin', I guess, pulled his rig across the driveway, and ol' Sinner skidded, turned on a dime, and headed back up toward the house under full throttle, clean over the hide-a-bed and end table the missus wanted me to get and charged pell-mell right into the garage where the ladies' auxiliary was wrappin' foil around the last of the pie and countin' up their proceeds.

"Well, hell, you'd think the sight of all those stone-faced Lutheran ladies aligned plumb like fence posts of piety across that table with all those pies would-a been a deterrent—it would-a deterred me, I tell ya, but ol' Sinner's ears was up, and he was snortin' fire by that time, havin' been pursued for so long and those hooves was rattlin' and sparkin' against the gravel, and he just charged hell-bent right into that den of righteousness, in one door and out the other—well, hell, the muffin tins flew one way, and loose change was rainin' down like a hailstorm, and clumps of apples and cherries and lemon meringue and styrofoam cups was flyin' and sworlin' around ever which way, and by the time it was over, those little ol' ladies looked like they'd been in a *seement* mixer full of pie and jello. You want to see a hissie fit, I tell ya, you'd a thought a whole harvest crew had walked across their clean kitchen floor. They was brandishin' forks and spatulas and pie tins and even comin' perilously close to takin' the name of the Lord in vain—all because of the shenanigans of the *men,* and they would say it the way they said *dirt* when they cleaned for company, and I'd bet the farm that ol' Sinner, if his preference been known, would-a voted for the glue factory right then and there."

Farley muttered something, shook his head, and checked his watch as Leo took a sip of his beer, then set it beside the others standing like a hedgerow across the table. He leaned back again and locked his hands behind his head. He looked like an eagle about to fly.

"Well," he said, "they finally got the son of a bitch cornered, back in there between the barn and the loading chute, and the boys that hadn't got disgusted with it all or been led home by their wives formed a big ol' half circle, kinda like a rabbit hunt, stretchin' from one side of the barn to the fence on the other, kind of a makeshift Powder River deal, just a big ol' half circle shoulder to shoulder and they just kept easin' in and closin' the circle on ol' Sinner; and as they drew up closer they started hummin' and singin' (*Faith of Our Fathers,* Carl said) and sort of mumblin' what they couldn't remember, but mumblin' tunefully and I'll be dammed if it didn't seem to gentle that crazy son of a bitch down.

"It may a shamed 'im, I couldn't say, surrounded by all those tunefully mumbling men, but he just seemed to drop his head, and those ears curled and wilted like corn in the heat of the day, and I'll be damned if he didn't start to pawin' and whinnyin' like he'd completely lost his spunk. All that vim and vinegar just drained out like hot oil, and he whinnied like he was tryin' to join in with that mumblin' choir of men and then I swear he began to tremble, and when that circle of tunefully mumbling men closed in, he just slunk back into the gate like a prodigal son.

"And I'll be damned if they no more had the gate closed than the Colonel, he started up again like nothin' ever happened. Just started braggin' that horse up again, even claimed it was so gentle and well broke that grandma and baby sister could ride 'im. Claimed a man could rope off 'im, hunt with 'im, plow with 'im, ride 'im in parades on the Fourth of July and then started it off at fifteen-hundert like nothin' had happened."

"Twelve, I believe," Carl said.

"Well, hell, it was like throwin' a goddamn rock down a goddamn well to China!

"But the Colonel he keeps cajolin' and braggin' and then slidin' down, auctioning assbackward, *now nine,* he says, *then eight-and-a-hav-now-eight-who'll give me seven-now-Boys,*

*Boys!* he scolds, and then talks that ol' Sinner up again, and the whole time that rodeo contractor he's hangin' back, mindin' his time, still workin' that toothpick. Hell, it must a been gold!

"He just stood there tall as a windmill, looking out from under that big ol' hat with those eyes as dry as rock salt, like the whole deal was preordained, and he was just waitin' for the dust to settle. Finally, the Colonel he gets down to one-fifty, and I guess the contractor he nodded or blinked or somethin'—I'll be damned if I caught it. It was like tryin' to see the wind, but the Colonel said *sold* and nodded his way, and he was getting' ready to load, goin' after that nice rig of his, and it all would-a been over, just a regular auction, when that ol' gal stepped out of the crowd. I don't know who she was or where she come from. Must a been there the whole time and gone unnoticed. Damned if I know, but she was one of those gals with her name on the back of her belt (*Gloria,* Carl said) and those fancy high boots and those tight jeans tucked inside. She looked too rough to be a woman and too clean to be a man. I don't know where the hell she come from."

"You get all kinds," Farley said.

"But I'll be damned if she didn't step into that circle and start tearin' into us like a bunch of heathens, and in no uncertain terms. I mean she tore into us, said that horse (*Creature, she called it,* Carl said.) was a victim of neglect half its life and hard ridin' the other half, like she knew what she was talkin' about, and the last thing that poor ol' creature needed was a strap around its nuts (*Oysters,* Carl said. *She called 'em oysters.*) and spurs in its ribs, and I could see a couple of the boys sort of wince at that and sag back a little, though it seemed to excite a couple of them, though I wouldn't want to say who they were.

"Anyway, she went on rantin' and ravin', claimin' she'd been shut out of the bidding, and I'll be damned if she didn't take off her hat, that nice brown felt hat with those Indian beads around the crown and that peacock feather stickin' up like a lightning rod. I guess she wanted us all to pitch in and save ol' Sinner from a life of brocin' in the rodeo, bein' made a spectacle of, she claimed, like men had made a spectacle of everything and that fancy hat of hers makin' the rounds might as well a been a collection plate for the devil—no one wanted it and they couldn't wait to get rid of it. A few of the boys made a show of opening their wallets and staring inside and shaking their heads like they was starin' into darkness, or pulled out a dollar or two just to be polite and avoid trouble and the whole time that Gal (*Gloria,* Carl said) kept a haranguin' us about the tragic life of that creature and its wretched existence at the hands of man and the worser life ahead of it if we didn't do somethin' about it right now, and I'll be damned if she didn't sound just like a preacher, in fact more like a preacher than the preachers we get nowadays, it seems. Hell, she made it sound like we was a part of one of those goddamned cult deals, and the whole time that contractor is easin' his rig back to load ol' Sinner, that pure white GMC with those dual wheels and cab behind the seat and chrome wheels sparklin' in the sunlight, idling with the sweetest little hum, and that horse trailer big as a dance hall, just easin' on back like nothin' is happenin', and then that ol' gal gets her hat back (*Gloria,* Carl said) and counts out the bills and loose change and apparently it's shy of the one-fifty the contractor already bid, so I'll be damned if she doesn't take off that fancy ring she's wearin' (*Genuine turquoise,* Carl said) and pitches it in the hat with the loose change and hands it over to the Colonel as casual as you please; but the

Colonel, hell, after forty years of auctioneering never run into anything like this before, just shook his head and said sorry ma'am, the biddin's closed, but that ol' gal gave him a tongue lashin' I'll never forget, the kind of thing that used to just go on behind closed doors. Right there in front of everyone, and the whole time the contractor he's backin' up that gooseneck rig, and the crowd parts for 'im like the Red Sea, and that ol' gal she goes up to ol' Sinner, just sashays up to him with her hand out sweet talkin' and clicking her tongue, callin' it baby, and that poor goddamned horse just stood there and lowered its head then raised it and stared. I tell ya I never seen a horse look so bewildered before. I tell ya, he was one bewildered son of a bitch. He didn't know which was worse, being rode hard or being insulted, and I'll be damned if his eyes didn't shift back and forth from the contractor to that gal; and then the contractor, he shut off the truck and took a rope out of the side of the trailer and marched back toward the corral, and just as that ol' horse was stickin' his nose out to inspect that gal's hand, that contractor's loop fluttered up in the air, as beautiful a loop as you'll ever see a man throw. It just seemed to hang up there in the air for an eternity, in that perfect circle, like a goddamned halo, just hoverin' over ol' Sinner's head for the longest time and everything stopped, years it seemed, and the man and the woman and the horse looked like somethin' chiseled from stone, like somethin' you'd see in a myoo-seum.

"But then the loop fell, just slick as shit, it dropped over Sinner's ears and head and snapped taut, and Sinner, he snorted and reared back, staggered on his hind legs, and I'll be damned if that gal didn't grab for the rope as the contractor took up the slack so they each had a hold of the rope, and ol' Sinner he was rearin', full of spunk, fightin' for his life again, and the contractor and the gal (*Gloria,* Carl said) was pullin' back and forth on it. Looked like one of those ol' railroad cars that men used to pump. Back and forth they pulled, and I tell ya, it's a damn good thing the Ladies' Auxiliary was still up in the garage cleanin' up. Spared a few coronaries that way. I tell ya there wasn't nothin' those two didn't call each another, and then the contractor he lost his hat as they wrestled, and she stomped on it in the dirt and rubbed it in the thistles, and horseshit and it wasn't long before they was both on the ground, sworlin' up dust and sweat and snarlin' and rippin' at clothes and hissin' and clawin' and kneein' and gnashin' and rollin' around in the dust and the thistles and shit, and I'll be damned if the Colonel he didn't try to start up the auction again on that dryrot ol' saddle by claimin' it was a genuine antique, and up by the house folks was loadin' up the last of the furniture and the Ladies' Auxiliary was sayin' the Benediction and gathering up the loose change, and ol' Elmer was leaning against a fencepost, smiling like there was no tomorrow. The widow, Aggie herself, was in the Nursing Home, dying, I imagine, while her estate was being sold, and all around us in the fields already Heartland Ag had its overhead sprinklers already creepin' across the fields, throwin' down rain even though there wasn't a cloud in the sky—and the whole entire time, us boys just wantin' to visit a little with some neighbors over a hot cup of coffee and a little homemade cherry pie on an August afternoon, maybe find us a little shady spot and shoot the breeze a little and count it a blessing to go home with a good deal on a set of sockets or roll of wire—and here we was witnessin' war!

"I tell ya, it's come down to a sorry state of affairs." Leo leaned forward, took off his hat and inspected the crease.

His arms rested on his knees as he kept turning that soiled, brittle hat over and over in his hands.

"Who won?" Farley asked. "Who got the horse anyway?"

Leo laughed. "Hell, no one. Not a single soul."

"That ol' horse was about as bewildered and dumbfounded as some of the rest of us. It tossed his head a couple of times and trembled and quivered like it was a goner anyway and hardly worth fightin' over. Hell, I think it was embarrassed 'bout the whole deal and wanted nothin' more than to retreat back like the rest of us and nose out some good green grass, if any was still to be had. It backed up a couple a steps, like a ropin' horse, and then it seemed to realize that in all the commotion and the feudin', the rope it had gone slack as an ol' man's peter and so ol' Sinner, he wheeled again and lit out north, busted right through the gate and headed out across the pasture, lopped the north fence and flud up the hill toward Turk's Bluff, fleein' for his life.

"Hell, last I seen of 'im he was just a speck on the hillside."

"I'll be damned," Farley said. "Broke free?"

"Yes, sir!" Leo said. "He's a free sinner now."

"They'll catch 'im." Carl said. "He can't run loose like that forever."

"I'll be damned," Farley said. "They just got feudin' and forgot about what they was fightin' over?"

"I guess they had a history of it," Leo said. "Used to be married before they had a partin' of the ways. I guess they never did hitch too well."

"A man never can tell about love and horses," Farley said.

"No, sir!" Leo said. "I did salvage me a piece of cherry pie up there in the garage though, before the ladies cleaned up. It wasn't much for looks, but it was still purty tasty."

Leo put his hat back on and pulled the brim down low over his eyes to shield them from the bright lights that burst into the room. He squinted at Marge coming across the floor, turning chairs upside down on the tables. "Your time's up, boys," she said. Carl counted the empty cans, multiplied and divided on that little black calculator he carried in his shirt pocket as Leo dropped a handful of bills on the table.

Outside, where they were chased by the closing of the bar, the late summer was still warm and mild, and the air carried the weight of that tight, seasonal ripeness. On the other side was the descent into fall.

Leo drove off, but Carl and Farley lingered for a moment beside their cars. In the silence, Farley listened for the hooves of a horse, like a racing heartbeat, in the dark hills north above the faint yellow dome of the lights of Paradise.

"You s'pose there's any truth to any of that?" Farley asked.

Carl shook his head and tapped his calculator in the palm of his hands. "The facts was all wrong," he said. "That's all I know." But beyond that he wouldn't say.

# She Would Offer Those Distant Men Buttermilk and Bread

*The band of flames bent across the hills like the teeth of a saw, flared in the tall bunch grass, tumbled down into a hollow of blue stem, vanished for half an hour then flared up again where it crested a hill closer to home.*

*From the north window of the kitchen she watched and marveled at the bright orange sky and black smoke drifting over the face of the crescent moon. She'd already threaded moist towels under the door and then drawn up the butter from the well, just in case. A kettle of lye was cooling on the stove.*

*Against the backdrop of flames she could see the dark outline of yoked oxen plowing a fireguard and the silhouettes of the men and boys, swinging sacks and shovels, and even hear, at times, their strong, urgent voices. She fingered the brooch around her neck, untied her hair and shook it loose around her shoulders, praying for a respite from silence, and then forgiveness of the pleasure she sought.*

*It was the voices that thrilled her. A month ago, in her loneliness, she had walked fifteen miles in the dry heat just to glimpse a wagon train of Mormons seeking a parched land further west. Downwind in the tall prairie grass she had crouched like a predator seeking those voices, the voices of men commanding the mules, "Gee!" and the voices of women calling their children and the children singing and protesting until the wagons creaked up over a bluff and vanished into the yellow sun.*

*To conceal her weakness and sadness, she'd brought back gooseberries she'd picked in a draw and then baked a pie for her husband, who feared she'd been kidnapped.*

*Again she sought forgiveness for the pleasure she took in the flames and for her desire that when they were extinguished the fighters would descend from the hill, sooty and tired and pleased, and she would hear the scuff of boots on the floor, the clearing of a throat, and she would offer those distant men buttermilk and bread; and, maybe, maybe they would speak of the homeland and their wives and children, even their hard lives, and join in grace, and then if tears came to her eyes, she could say it was the acrid air.*

# A Stone House of Many Rooms

On a Sunday that had eased into a hot summer night, Carl knelt in a bed of fallen rose petals, crisp and shriveled as dried fruit, as he waited for Delores Denning's porch light to come on.

He peered through the twining branches, the leafy mosaic of shrubs in the side yard, alert to footsteps that might be coming down the sidewalk, voices that might rise out of the shadows of the elms, or the bright flush of headlights from a passing car.

He crouched lower, a shadow among shadows, as he felt a warm surge of shame that he instantly denied to himself. Argued it away. It was only information that he was after. Only information. Nothing more than that. Just information. What was the term they used on the news? He bowed his head so it almost touched his knees. A thorn scratched his forehead. A fact-finding mission! That was it. A fact-finding mission. He was on a fact-finding mission.

And his mission had brought him here, to this stone house on the end of Main Street, hoping that Delores Denning, the only person in Paradise of whom nothing was known, would come out on her porch so he could appear, nonchalant, on a summer stroll, nod a greeting, comment on how sticky the night was, how pesky the mosquitoes were—the worst in seven years—and one thing would lead to another, and then he, Carl Spurney, the unofficial historian of Paradise could excavate the facts of Delores Denning's life, and from that learn if she was, as he believed, the heroine in the salesman's story. The woman who made a pillow of stone.

The journey that had brought him here, kneeling in the shadows and the fallen rose petals, had begun last winter when a blizzard had forced a retreat from everyday life, held folks inside for long games of canasta and Scrabble, and brought the comfort of a cold obscurity to town.

The whistle of tires on the icy streets was a siren call for men to shoulder a car from the curb or shovel out a driveway. All over town folks struggled to free one another. The snow obscured the harsh lines of businesses and the pitched roofs of churches, the stark branches of leafless elms. In the curvature of the snow, the houses were linked like ocean waves. The snow unified things, brought things together. The snow did that. It brought out a warmth in people.

In kitchens and hallways the odor of damp gloves, mittens, boots, and overcoats stirred a warm nostalgia that fused with the present as laconic voices arose out of memory, blended over cups of steaming coffee and warm cinnamon rolls, while the old-timers of Paradise dreamed up tales of fierce storms and enormous snowdrifts that swallowed barns, houses, and windmills and forced epic solitary treks for help across the white wastelands. Yes sir! There was *weather* back then.

Even strangers to Paradise were transformed by the snow.

One such man was an insurance salesman whose territory was the heartland. Before the storm claimed him, he was loud and agitated, quick with a forced laugh and joke, and often generous as a way of drawing attention to his prominence. He wore expensive alligator boots and boasted that his gold wristwatch cost more than most folks' houses.

When he drank scotch at the Greener Pasture or ate sirloin at the M & P Cafe he picked up the tab for others, ordered refills, and told stories as if he had returned from exploring the New World. He told of scorching infidelities, blood feuds, abandoned children, corruption in high places, and huge profits harvested by the ruthless and self-serving—but they were all familiar tales, even to the folks of Paradise, things seen on television or on the covers of the magazines and newspapers at the grocery store. It was like the gossip of a small town without the bond of a borrowed cup of sugar.

Then on the evening of the third day of the storm, the snow finally subdued even his spirit. A change came over the salesman while Carl, a few seats down at the counter of the M & P Cafe, lingered over his Friday night coffee and orange sherbet. The sherbet, he'd already figured, would put him right at two thousand calories for the day. In another fifteen minutes he would be home—in time to catch the news, the weather, take his bath during the sports and be in bed by 10:45, ready for page 639, "Diverticulitis," in the *Merck Manual,* ninth edition.

Joanna was setting chairs upside down on the tables and mopping up puddles of melted snow. Outside the snow still slanted in from the north before a fierce wind. The salesman's hands encircled his cup, and he'd been silent for a long time. The coffee in his cup was cold. When he finally spoke, his voice and the story seemed to come out of nowhere.

It was a story about a beautiful young woman who had married a handsome young man. "A prince," she thought, "a regular prince."

"Hell, it was a fairy tale," the salesman said. "A goddamned fairy tale. At least in the beginning.

"She was some kinda gal, I guess. Cute as a peach and she just kept gettin' purtier and purtier all the time. After a while I guess her husband started gettin' spooked by it. Hell, everywhere they went—out for supper, a high school basketball game, a church potluck, just anywhere—it seemed that men was always sneakin' looks at her, findin' excuses to get close to her. He could only imagine what it was like when he wasn't around.

"And what made matters worse was that he swore she seemed to kinda glow a little more than usual, shine a little bit like a waxed-up car, all polished up with the sunlight reflectin' off her.

"Well, hell it wasn't long before he didn't want to take her out at all. Kept her home with all sorts of excuses, which of course only served to make matters worse. I guess she started inventing excuses to get out of the house, get all dolled up, and the more she did that the more he got suspicious.

"Love is a mighty strange thing, I tell ya. It can sure as hell bring out the worst in folks, sometimes."

He checked his watch, glanced out the window at the driving snow. "If it keeps on like this I might end up a citizen of your town," he told Joanna. "You'll have to make room in the cemetery for me."

"It's not the worst winter we've had," she said, not even looking at Carl.

"Nineteen hundred and fifty-two," Carl said. "Seventy-three inches of snow from December through the end of April. The Union Pacific couldn't even run for two months."

"Carl, there, he's our local history expert. If he don't know it, it didn't happed."

She squeezed out the mop in the sink behind the counter. "He runs the accountant office across the street. Does my books for me and just 'bout everyone else's in town for that matter."

"I just push a pencil," Carl said, "try to make things balance." He scraped the bowl of his sherbet with quick little swipes of the spoon.

"I suppose they didn't stay married too long?"

The salesman looked down the counter, surprised, as if seeing Carl for the first time. As if this slight, neat man in a sport shirt and gray cardigan and brown trousers had just arrived.

"He started beatin' on her I guess. Pretty bad. At least that's what my brother-in-law told me. He's the sheriff in Wichita."

"She must a still been fairly young and quite the looker?"

The salesman took out his checkbook and tapped it in the palm of his hand. "Yes sir," he said. "Yes sir.

"One thing finally led to another, and she just up and left him one night, couldn't take it any longer. But he was a persistent bastard, I guess, and found her and wouldn't give her any peace. He just kept after her no matter where she went. Just pestered her to death, I guess. Even pulled a gun on her one night and threatened to kill her right there and then."

He shook his head and tapped the checkbook in his palm, then held it for a moment. "I tell you, love does some mighty strange things to folks."

"That don't sound like love to me," Joanna said, emptying the till, spreading out the bills and change on the counter.

"You can argue with me if you want to," the salesman said, "but I'd maintain that it's all love. The good and the bad.

It's like weather, I figure. Rain, drought, snow, no matter, it's all weather. I think love's like that."

"Not in my book," Joanna said, stacking the twenties. "I just want the sunny days, the good weather. You can have the rest."

"She must of taken out a restraining order?" Carl asked.

"Don't know. The brother-in-law didn't say, but I'm sure she sure as hell wanted him as far away as she could 'im."

"Fifty percent of the time, restraining orders are taken out in cases like that," Carl said.

"Well, if they did, it must of not been of much use, because she couldn't find any peace of mind from him."

"I saw a TV show on stalkin'," Joanna said, "a news show. They got laws now."

Carl nodded, but before he could speak the salesman went on.

"I don't know about the details, but here's the kicker. The real clincher.

"My brother-in-law says they locked her up. In jail no less. Yep, that's right. In jail. It wasn't him but her they finally locked up. For her own protection, I guess. It was the only place they could be sure he couldn't get at her.

"Hell, Frank said, that's the brother-in-law, Frank. Frank said she just sagged down in that jail like a heap of clothes. Like nine months or so of fear was all that had held her up. Like fear was her skeleton. So as soon as she felt safe and sound in that jail she just collapsed like an empty gunnysack. There was nothin' to hold her up anymore.

"It was the damnedest thing, I guess, and ol' Frank, that's the brother-in-law, he married my second sister, Arlene, he said she just ran her finger along those little grooves between the cinder blocks and fell asleep with her head against the stone wall like it was the softest pillow on God's green earth.

It was the damnedest thing, he said, and I swear there was a little lump in his throat when he told me, and he's a big man, too."

He stopped tapping his checkbook and threw a twenty dollar bill down on the counter. "I'll get the coffee and sherbet, too," he said. "I try to stay on the good side of accountants. I tell ya, folks do the strangest things for love."

"I still say that ain't love," Joanna said, shoving the money into a bank bag.

"Would you call that love?" she asked Carl.

"I work with numbers. I don't know if I would or not. I'd need to know more. Need more facts." He pushed his empty coffee cup to the edge of the counter and wiped up a stain with his napkin. He felt a cool breeze sweep along the floor and ease up his pants leg. Outside it was too white to even see across the street. He thought he saw some boys on a sled rush by on the sidewalk, but it might have been a wishful thought—something to fill the white void.

On his way out, the salesman joked with Joanna about franchising her pie and coffee and slapped Carl on the back. "I'd change from term to whole life, if I was you," he said, handing Carl a business card.

At home Carl hung his coat over a heating duct and realized that the night had slipped away—the news and weather had come and gone without him, a list of evening chores lay intact by the coffee pot, and he had missed his evening bath for the first time since high winds had knocked down power lines last spring, *April 17, it was,* and the next day in his office he kept drifting away from the IGA quarterlies. When he didn't appear at the cafe for 10:30 coffee, at the table by the window with the Seven Magnificent Geezers, his absence could only be explained as an act of God.

So Ivan Corman, testing his replaced hip, limped across the street to Carl's office at 10:45. Seeing Carl sitting upright in his chair and staring at a wall that held nothing but white paint was more alarming than his worst fears.

"We thought you'd died," Ivan said, limping into the office. "But you don't look dead to me. At least not completely dead."

When Carl finally crossed the street only two of the Seven Magnificent Geezers were still drinking coffee.

"You see what happens," Ivan said. "The others have already died off on us."

Again in the afternoon, the columns of figures kept fading away like the small lines on an eye chart, and into that gray-white space floated images of the woman in the salesman's story. There were facts that Carl needed to know—age and height and weight and hometowns and dates and times—everything the salesman, in his vagueness, had left out, but Carl, mistrustful of his own imagination, couldn't put the story to rest without the facts, couldn't make it balance, even though he tried again and again with invented facts.

He worked on it even as the snow melted away except for a gray, dirty drift in the shade of the bank, and it occupied him through the cold rains and gray skies of a sloppy spring. He tried different ages, different shadings of hair and complexion, manner of walking, eyes blue or green or brown, a head tilted or flush with the world, but nothing seemed right.

In March, for the first time in twenty-three years, he missed choir practice on a Thursday night, and in April, he missed the Wednesday night roast beef special at the cafe.

By late spring, the Seven Magnificent Geezers, holding council over their coffee, were seeking explanations to the change they'd witnessed. They stirred their coffee and agreed that he had a screw loose someplace, that was for sure. *He's just not quite all there anymore. Yes sir. He might have that Alzheimer's deal. It can cut you down in the prime of life. There's no tellin'. He's sixty-two if he's a day. No! Yes sir, sixty-two. You betcha. Graduated high school the same year as Irene. I'll be darned. Yes sir*—but then they couldn't agree on the graduation date for Irene.

Then one day in May, Carl was sitting at the table with the Seven Magnificent Geezers, waiting for his coffee to cool, measuring out a teaspoon of sugar, when Delores Denning entered the cafe, and when Carl saw her, it was like finding a missing receipt or a check that explained an imbalance. To his eye she walked as if beneath her a thin sheet of ice groaned and cracked; her hunched shoulders and bowed head, he believed, were a shield for some soft, vulnerable spot at her core.

He wondered about her age, her hometown, if she worked or had family as she paid for a cup of coffee in a styrofoam cup.

As soon as she was out the door the Seven Magnificent Geezers confirmed that she was new in town and a pretty odd duck who kept to herself in the old Jenkins' place, and they reasoned that she probably had been jilted in love or was maybe a famous actress layin' low in a small town as she recovered from drug addiction, or maybe it was one of those witness protection deals, since Walt, at the post office, said he'd seen her pick up mail with other names on it. Names besides hers, Delores Denning.

One day at the IGA, in the canned goods aisle, Carl turned around with a small can of creamed corn in his hand and found himself face-to-face with her.

His eyes fell on a small indentation on her forehead, like a chip in a table, and then a longer, almost graceful, line on the side of her face, as if a tear had carved a shallow course as it ran down her cheek.

He fingered his tie, stammered to say his name, her name, excuse himself, nod and smile, but before he sorted it all out, made his choice, she was gone, down the aisle, picking up a can of tomato paste, and Carl was left alone, feeling the terror of words, longing for the comfort of numbers.

Again, one day at the bank, while turning in a roll of pennies, he'd found her in line behind him, but that time he'd managed a weak smile. A clear phrase, *Welcome to Paradise,* formed on his lips, but by then she was at the teller's window, her back to him, and the words floated and sunk like tiny seeds in a swift current.

For Carl, more and more, she became as elusive and bewildering as last night's dream. Unless immediately retrieved, the details vanished, yet the more carefully reconstructed, the less sense it made. Who was she? Who stood beside her? What was she doing here? She was the stranger in the dream.

So he'd written out the questions on a file card, and for three weeks practiced them while pacing in his office and living room. After he commented on the weather, one thing would lead to another until one by one the doors to Delores Denning's life would open, all the way back to that jail, to the terror, the dream of the marriage to the handsome prince. The fairy tale would have dates and times and places.

So now he waited, kneeling in the dried rose petals, for her porch light to come on. By Carl's watch it was 11:52 when the flickering blue light at the center of the house vanished, and then one by one the white lights behind each curtained window disappeared until only the light from a small, high window remained.

Behind him the entire town had retreated into the night, and only a few vague stars and a hazy half-moon held back the darkness. Night sounds from the country—from the hills to the north, beyond Turk's Bluff—began to filter into town. Young coyotes tested the dark silence while an owl sent up a question that trailed off into silence.

The erasure of the clean, clear lines of the day, roads and sidewalks and fence lines and power lines and the clear line of the horizon, the demarcation between heaven and earth left Carl edgy. Sometimes he felt something like a wild bird in his chest struggling to escape.

The rose petals and leaves crackled as he shifted his weight. The twining branches enclosed him in a cage, offered protection from the uncertainty of a world without order. He carefully bent a branch, peered between it and another one as a breeze he couldn't feel stirred the high branches of the maples behind the house. The branches sagged on the roof and the leaves swept against the shingles.

Then the entire house was suddenly pitched into darkness, and the final order imposed on the day vanished. He felt the edge of the file card in his palm, rehearsed the questions until a screen door banged, rattled, and a silhouette appeared in the doorway, drifted toward the front steps as a few fireflies in the yard brought relief to the darkness.

Carl waited for the porch light, shifted his weight in the dried petals and leaves, leaned forward on his knees, gathered his feet under him.

He thought, *let there be light, let there be light* as he peered through the bars around him.

On the porch a scratching friction erupted into a tiny white flame that seemed to mock his desire. The small flame lit a cigarette, illuminating a smooth face, bare white shoulders, and fragments of arms, elbows, knees, breasts—flesh in kaleidoscopic rotation falling apart then reforming over and over in a dream as elusive and profound as the stasis of last winter's snow.

There was a hush, and then an elongated exhalation of breath as the bright image of flesh, perhaps in memory now, pulsed in and out of the darkness as the orange glow of a cigarette skittered up and down.

The edge of the card cut across his palm as he squeezed. His pale forearm ached as he crumpled the card into a ball.

On the porch the woman, secure in the darkness, heard a trivial noise in the side yard but dismissed it as the creak of branches or maybe the rustling of a small rodent. When she finished her cigarette, she rose and stretched her arms toward the vaporous half-moon, arched her back, then snapped her hair over her shoulder to dry in the warm summer air.

If Carl had still been watching, he could have seen her beauty, silver as a fish in the moonlight, but he was bent down, slouched, retreating deeper into his concealment, his thoughts seeking refuge in the order of the day, the straight, clean streets, the clear horizon, the Fabric Store account, the laundry, the milk he needed from the store. He could count on coffee with the Seven Magnificent Geezers at 10:30 and 3:30, the roast beef special at the M & P, choir practice on Thursday night.

When Delores Denning reentered her dark house, Carl shoved the crumpled card deep into the pocket of his trousers. It rubbed against his leg, bulged like a wound, as he passed the cafe, the hardware store, the bank, his own office, drifting down Main Street like an apparition who becomes the subject of stories told in winter, who haunts the place from which he comes.

## The Flood

*Before Ike built the dams they said she prayed for rain. And her prayers were answered, on April the 19th, the 22nd, the 29th; and her prayers were answered again in the first week of May and again on the 15th and 23rd and the first of June until the water coursed down from the hills, filled the ditches, overran the road, then channeled across the fields and poured into the river.*

That water has a mind of its own, *he said, when it rose back up out of the river and spread over the tender corn and turned the ripe wheat into a blackened, tangled mat of witch's hair.*

*When it came up the stairs of the root cellar, she filled the bushel basket full of her canned preserves, last summer's beans and tomatoes, and carried them straight to the second floor of the house, so by late afternoon, the bedroom was filled with mason jars, sacks of grain, potatoes and onions, and then a crate full of fryers and twelve piglets wrested from the sow, who she said would just have to fend for herself; but she, too, finally found her way to the second story, ascended the stairs and sprawled out, grunting, while she nursed her young beside the oak vanity.*

Who says you can't take it with you, *she told her husband, who was content to sit tight, let it take what it would and leave what it would.* We could afford some cleanin' out, I s'pose, *he said.*

*By the second day, the water was up to the porch and then into the house, and by evening, it was the level of the kitchen table so they stayed upstairs, and her husband sat by the window, smoking a pipe and gazing across the wide band of water, and tried to recollect the debris floating by, as if recreating the world before the flood.*

That'd be Virgil's granary, *he'd say at the sight of a red plank bobbing on the water.*

*Then he got out his fishing pole, baited the hook from a jar of pickles, and dropped in a line from the second-story window because he swore he could smell catfish in the water below. Toward evening he called to her when off in the distance he saw his neighbor's chicken coop bobbing in a tangled mesh of wire and posts, and on the roof, there, like a weather vane, stood that surly ol' boar that was always getting' out and rootin' in the cornfield.*

A flood does have its advantages, *he said.*

*When a neighbor with an oar and mattress came by, she said,* we intend to ride it out, God willing; if the house goes I go with it, *she said, and by evening of that day when the water began to recede she went downstairs to the kitchen and began rilling the water with a broom so the mud wouldn't settle. She said,* I got no desire to plant a garden right in my very own kitchen.

*He watched from the dry stairs, aroused at the sight of her dress rolled to her waist, the white flesh of her legs like the silt of flour against the opaque surface of the flood; a small muddy wave leapt up between her thighs and then coursed back down in dark sinuous streams.*

*As she stirred the water, he harbored that image, tucked it away, like a boat moored in a storm, and that night with the sounds of the water slapping against the siding and cascading back down the steps of the porch; at midnight amidst the soft clucking of the chickens and the deep, satisfied rumblings of the sow and the pleading squeals of the small, pink swine he mounted her as he had years ago, and she sighed,* Oh God, in the midst of plagues; *and when she heard the rattling of the mason jars around the bed, all her preserves, she moaned,* what next, *and then she swore she felt the house slip from its foundation and she feared she was floating away, borne on that water, bound for an eternity of the same.*

# Grounded

It was late and Thanksgiving was near and April, unaware of the chill in the air, was in the backyard chasing the last of the falling leaves.

Without design she had escaped the house, the chores her parents had given her while they went to the store. The escape had begun when she was making her bed and a piece of a jigsaw puzzle, an elephant's trunk, fell from the pink comforter, so she'd abandoned her half-made bed to find the elephant with the missing trunk.

The elephant had eluded her, but under her bed she'd found a strawberry doll, missing for thousands of years, a piece of licorice stashed in a box of crayons, a battery for her radio, a token for a board game, and a thousand-million-zillion dollars of Monopoly money.

One thing always led to another with her, so when she'd seen some squirrels scurrying along a high wire in the backyard beyond the patio, she'd wandered outside, and when a leaf, dry as a saltine, had caught in her hair, crumbled in her grasp, she'd looked up at a sky full of leaves, like summer moths, and begun lurching after one and then another, trying to catch one for each of the years she would live.

She had counted to 117 when she heard the noise of an engine, the creaking of a door, and those distant, adult voices. Thinking it was her parents and remembering her chores, she brushed the leaves from her shoulders and shook out her hair and was about to sprint back into the house before she was seen and then grounded to her room and an evening of practicing the flute, or spelling or math; her room, with the door closed, was not yet a refuge, and seemed awfully small to her then, even though her friends thought her house was the best house in Paradise and maybe the whole entire world because her father was rich and it was new and on the outskirts of town and had a big-screen TV and a pool and a trampoline in the backyard.

But the engine, the low voices she heard, came from next door, beyond the cedar fence, the privacy fence, her mother called it. They were men's voices and they called out to Malcolm, who lived there, tending to a garden and animals in the pasture behind the house. A board was warped in the fence, and through the narrow slit she could spy on him, on the steer and pig nosing the grass, or the white chickens pecking and scratching. It was like a page in a storybook.

Sometimes she would pitch an apple or a sandwich she was supposed to eat over the fence. The chickens squawked and fled, but the steer and pig were curious, always curious. Once she saw Malcolm pushing a red wheelbarrow through the vertical light of her view, and more than anything she wanted to ride in that red wheelbarrow and watch the white chickens scatter and squawk as she bounced across the pasture.

Sometimes when her parents were gone, she'd call out to him, telling him about a skinned knee she'd suffered in first grade or a Disney movie she'd seen, and he'd come over and slip a piece of gum through the crack in the fence, but she never told her parents because they complained about the odors of compost and leaves, worried about sanitation, the flies when they barbecued, the tall grass, mosquitoes and manure, and said they would be happy when the grandfather clauses expired.

Now she pressed close to the fence, out of curiosity, forgetting her room and the falling leaves and the years of her life. She aligned her eye in the narrow slit where the board was warped. Her nose flattened against the rough boards and the flesh on her cheek molded itself to the grain. Even though her mother was gone, April could hear her voice, warning about splinters.

Beyond the fence she saw a bright red truck, high and enclosed in back, with some letters painted on the side. Words to her then would either float by like clouds or settle like a coin in the palm of her hands. *Fast* and *clean* she understood, but *efficient* eluded her like the elephant of the puzzle, lost forever in the clutter of her room.

Then two men, one lean, with a mustache and a blue stocking cap, and one older, smooth-faced, with a white, red-stained apron stepped from the truck as Malcolm entered the light. He was smiling and wearing a plaid coat that hung to his thighs, down almost to his high rubber boots. As they talked their breath floated up like cartoon bubbles, and even though they smiled and laughed, there was a distance, a reserve about them. Some duty on their minds. Their hands sought tools, boots and aprons, and then the lean man with the stocking cap reached into the truck and pulled out a rifle, bolted in a shell, *click-click*, and without another word began walking gingerly across the pasture. To April he looked like a man trying to move without moving, like the wind or a limb on a tree. As she pressed closer to the fence, she felt her breath stopping deep in her chest, like a yo-yo dying at the end of a string.

He stopped about twenty feet from the grazing steer and slowly raised the rifle when he whistled. The steer's thick white face rose, turned slowly toward the noise, curious as it chewed the long stems of tasseled grass.

The shot snapped, echoed in the heavy air, and the steer collapsed, thumped against the ground. The sound traveled along the ground like a deep drum, vibrated up through April's feet just as she flinched from the shot. She felt it and heard it at the same time, and then the steer's head arched and rocked, its rear legs stiffened and its flanks thrust in the air.

Without a word, in this new immense silence, the older man, with the smooth face and kindly manner, walked casually up to the steer, stooped, and with a quick thrust and pull released the warm blood from the white neck. As the blood gushed onto the cold ground a ghostly mist rose from the red pool.

Then the lean man joined him for the quick work of knives, gutting the steer like a huge fish, severing the hooves and head and tail, peeling the hide like a rubber glove, until what remained was impossible to link with what had been there grazing in the pasture a few moments before.

They drove the truck up to the steaming carcass, then with a whir of a lift, hoisted it in the air. In the young man's hands a chain saw sputtered, revved, then roared against the silence, splitting the marble carcass, making two of what was one. Still, there was a muscle on the shiny cream-colored flank that twitched like a muscle in April's leg, at night, when she was trying to sleep.

Then the lean man with the rifle circled the truck and headed toward the pen where the pig waited to be let out. At the sight of the rifle poking into the pen, the pig grunted and raised its head. Its jowls bobbed up and down, its snout rose, and its mouth opened, and then the same hallow snap echoed in the air, followed by a squeal and then the thrashing and thumping of death throes as the lean man with the drawn knife stepped over the fence. Again the scent of fresh blood was added to the air.

It took both of the butchers, struggling with the dead weight and the slippery blood on their hands, to carry the pig to the truck. They rolled it onto a rack, its stiff legs pointing up, its head lolling over the edge.

They were quick and clean with the pig too, leaving only a red-purple stain on the ground beside the truck, and then the big door with *Fast, Efficient, Clean* in big red letters, rolled down, and the men wiped the blood from their knives, leaned the gun against the tire, folded their aprons and washed their hands at the truck's water tank. Malcolm joined them with a pitchfork in his hands. Even his black rubber boots were stained with something that looked like blood.

The three men lingered in silence for a long time beside the truck, but when they finally spoke there was an easy patter to their voices, like the rhythm of slow rain on the roof. They nodded, looked down at their boots, at the ground, one toed a pebble to the left and right, and then they looked up at one another and exchanged an easy word or two that didn't seem to intrude upon the silence but nestled into it, became a part of it.

The older one had a thermos of coffee, and the steam rose over his face as he drank, holding the plastic cup like a chalice, while the young one lit a cigarette and cocked his leg against a tire of the truck, listened and nodded as Malcolm leaned on his pitchfork and gestured across the pasture with a gloved hand.

All around them steam rose from the pools of blood, from their own breath, from coffee and cigarettes. A few magpies skittered along the ground, pecked at the blood-stained grass. They squawked and scolded, rose to the branches of the cottonwood then dove back down to the ground. Then the white chickens discovered the moist red earth and fanned out along the ground.

All of this is offered to April in the pale light of autumn, within a frame afforded by the warp in the fence, and it lingers in a larger frame of a pasture surrounded on three sides by houses, pitched roofs and swooping lines of high wires and tall posts and on another by a grid of roads and ordered fields stretching out to the falling sun.

She has stared so long that her eyes feel dry and fingers cold, way down to the ends, to the tips of her painted nails. When she shivers she is afraid her arms and legs may fall off like baggy clothes. She feels like she could shake out of her own skin and the autumn breeze could carry her away.

The world beyond the fence has captured her, holds her now in its sudden silence and immensity, even as the truck finally leaves and Malcolm, alone, begins to push a wheelbarrow and fork up the offal, turns over stock tanks and troughs, humming to himself as he puts things down for winter. It holds her like a dream even when she vaguely understands that the garage door has opened and her mother's voice is calling her to come inside. Calling from the house, from her cluttered room.

Calling her name.

*April.*

*April.*

*April.*

Her name with a period at the end, always a period, the end of a sentence, learned in school—calling her back inside. *Come in or be grounded,* orders the voice, her mother's voice, but April needs to know if her legs belong to her, if they will support her still, so she reaches up on the fence, clutches the two-by-four frame as her feet find the post. She shinnies and scrambles up and over the rough boards, careless about the splinters and burns on her bare hands, then scrambles over the top and leaps down into the pasture, falling at first to her knees, stumbling, then rising and running across the pasture, scattering the magpies and chickens in her wake, fleeing through the dappled light of the late afternoon like a swirling dervish of leaves.

Malcolm, beside the wheelbarrow, looks up and sees her for the first time, a chaos of knees and elbows and flopping blond hair.

"April!" he says.

By then she is in his arms, blowing up against him like a tumbleweed, her arms trying to encircle his waist as her cheek presses against his stomach, listening hard for his heart. His thick coat smells like autumn.

She giggles when she hears it, his heart, thumping like a drum, and then leans back and takes his hands in hers, the thick dark hands held by the thin, delicate white hands; she leans back, anchored by those hands as she spins and pulls him in a circle of her own design, dancing and giggling, orbiting around and around him, a moth in summer, the whirlwind of leaves in the fall.

## The Dugout

*From the dark oven where he was hidden the infant could hear the low, grave rumble of his father's voice and the quick scuff of his mother's feet against the dirt floor—a book and photograph slid between fabric, a brooch rattled into a tin cup, a kettle scraped across the cook-stove and then the sweet odor of yeast and milk and sweet potatoes vanished—and he knew, the infant knew, even then, that silence was a sanctuary.*

*In the outer room the flimsy wooden door creaked open, scraped against the floor; a horse whinnied, pawed, and then the low, guarded utterances of men, in English and Swedish and Kiowa, his father's and strangers', bartered, struck a deal, and the scent of bacon and molasses and horse blankets reached the concealed child.*

*Even when the hooves of the gaunt horses retreated across the prairie, and the oven door opened, and the pale light of the room reached his eyes, the child did not dare risk a sound.*

# Into This House

They were just boys, and it was spring, and they were driving around the countryside looking for something to shoot.

One of the boys, Craig, spit sunflower seeds out the window and watched the husks ride the wind. For a moment he wondered about the fate of a split seed, but the thought was quickly absorbed by the memories of the girl he had been with last night—the dry, desert scent of her hair, her milky voice—and the awful, enticing images of everything exploding into the sky like a cluster of fireworks. The stock of his gun, its barrel on the floorboard, bounced against his thigh. He dug into the bag for fresh seeds.

The other boy, Dwayne, drove the familiar gravel roads without looking; his eyes searched the fields for a target, found some doves on a high wire, but they started and scattered as he raised his rifle to the window.

"Shit," he grinned, relishing the chance to protest. He made the word sound like the unsheathing of a knife.

Together, separate from the adult world, they liked to talk as they had heard men talk, or imagined men to talk. Usually men when they were with men. Or men when they were drunk. At times it became a strutting caricature, especially for Dwayne, who at fifteen was a year older than his friend. They sometimes joked that they were brothers, but in truth, each knew little of the heart of the other. Both had the recurring dream of entering a large store full of fragile dishes and glassware, and being allowed, like the winner of a shopping spree, to smash everything in sight.

Dwayne took a Marlboro from the pack on the dash and lit it, flipped the match out the window and clenched the cigarette between his teeth. It was early afternoon and the air was still and heavy, and the humidity evoked the prospect of a fine, ripening sweat. A strange, new scent felt like it was about to burst from their flesh. It made them nervous and eager and scared, though they would not admit it. Instead they drove and hunted—for something, someplace—following a vague desire for some momentous event that resided in the next minute or glittered in the next field.

The car spun forward, threw gravel, then idled down as they scanned the fields of green silky wheat, the straight brown furrows of corn, the thick green stubble of alfalfa with its unfathomable roots. The fields were bordered by hedgerows of low and broken limbs entangled in last year's weeds.

They passed a farmer planting corn, intent on keeping his rows straight, but neither of them waved. The tractor and planter faded into the distance under a swirling cloud of seagulls that scattered and soared. Their white wings were brilliant against the brown earth.

"Get any last night?" Dwayne asked, the cigarette steady between his clenched teeth.

Craig split a sunflower seed between his teeth and explored the husk with the tip of his tongue before chewing up the seed. "Enough," he finally answered, knowing he would be taunted no matter how he answered.

The truth is that he didn't know what he'd gotten last night. Outside the girl's house in his father's Mercury, with the glare of the corner streetlight on the hood and flyspecks on the windshield, he'd cupped her small breast as she moaned and nibbled on his lips and then refused him with a longing that left him feeling lost in a dense fog. When she clasped the top of her blouse and ran up to the front porch, something warm had vanished like a breath. If asked, he wouldn't have known the color of her eyes.

"Shit, you didn't even dip a finger in the pie, did you?" Dwayne laughed. He punched Craig on the arm, flipped the cigarette out the window and boasted about having to give his little brother lessons in love.

Craig flushed enough to reward Dwayne, then gazed out the window as if searching for something to shoot, but it was a cover for retreat into the comfort of his own thoughts, like pulling a blanket over his face in the mornings. It was a way of filtering things. It was something he'd learned at home by closing his bedroom door.

Inside his room he could imagine anything without embarrassment or shame. Inside his room he could bring anything to life.

His fingers trailed over the smooth stock of the gun while he gazed across the empty fields. It was inside his room where he had brought this gun back to life.

He'd found it concealed by dust and cobwebs behind a stack of bald tires in the corner of the garage and then spent days sanding the nicks from the stock and scouring rust from the barrel. It was an "over-under," a combination .410 shotgun and .22 rifle, and Dwayne, when he heard about it, claimed it must be worth a fortune.

Then one night at dinner, his father, suffering under his mother's stern eyes, kept slicing pieces of chicken-fried steak into smaller and smaller pieces, eyeing each piece as if it were part of a puzzle, then chewing it slowly and drumming his fingers on the table. When he finished, he cleared his throat, but nothing came of it as he pushed himself up from the table and shuffled off to the den and turned on the news, leaving his mother, finally, with words as crisp and clean as the strokes she used in chopping carrots, to tell him that the gun he'd found and worked so hard to restore had once belonged to his Uncle Will, who was never quite all there and had used it to commit suicide, *and your father, just like he does everything, was supposed to get rid of it but he just stuck it in the corner of the garage like he does everything else and forgot about it.* She scrubbed the congealed grease from the skillet, rinsed it quickly under a stream of hot water, then squeezed her hands in a dish towel.

Down the road Dwayne fired into an abandoned house, through the dark opening of a doorway. The porch sagged, and shingles had rotted, curled, or blown off in a storm: fireweed, thistles, and sunflowers crowded the foundation, reclaiming what had once been neat and orderly like the farmer's rows of corn. Craig balanced the gun on the floorboard and wondered where the people had gone, the ones his parents identified with the Haskins' place or the Perkins' place or whatever. They were landmarks for his parents, a way to keep their bearings straight.

Turning south they entered a tunnel of cottonwoods that led to the abandoned Lutheran church, the only surviving building of a pioneer town. Shards of stained glass lay in piles beneath the large frame windows. Each shard contained a piece of a biblical scene—a fragment of a staff or a crown, a remnant of a shepherd's cloak, a lamb's face, a hand impaled on a cross. Barn swallows and pigeons dove into the dark opening of the building that was now their refuge. Dwayne raised his rifle out of the car window and fired at a swallow that emerged from the darkness and rose toward the blue sky. At the cemetery beside the church he fired at a meadowlark perched on a headstone. The shot ricocheted off a granite marker while the lark fidgeted, hopped, glanced about, then resumed its sweet song.

"Hell, they're just rocks with some names on them," Dwayne shrugged. "The dead guys won't mind." He grinned at Craig then fired again.

When they drove on, he took a can of Coors from the six-pack on the seat and clasped it between his thighs as he opened it. He exaggerated the satisfaction of the first sip and claimed that God had designed the crotch to hold a beer can while driving.

Later, when he stopped to piss, he arched a spectacular rainbow down upon the tadpoles in the ditch. The tadpoles swarmed around the sunken Coke and Quaker State cans in the weeds near the muddy bank. After Dwayne zipped up, he shouldered his .22 and fired at a dragonfly perched on a crimped can of Budweiser. Soon the water was splashing under a barrage of bullets.

Craig leaned back against the car and drank his beer and watched the cans skitter across the ditch. He stole a glance of himself in the side mirror and wished the girl he had been with last night could see him now. He pulled his baseball cap down to shield his eyes and let his shoulders sag in a cool, weary slouch. Under the shadow of his cap his face was smooth and inscrutable. There was nothing in his face to betray him. It was like closing the door to his room.

"Hey, dickhead! You ever goin' to fire that piece of yours?" Dwayne called without turning around. He was drawing a bead on a waterskipper.

"I'm saving myself," Craig said. But his words were lost in the gunfire and splash of water.

Back in the car they continued their wandering course from mile line to mile line, listening to Led Zeppelin and Jimi Hendrix, and then the Doors and bragging about the coyotes they would kill in the fall, laughing about the time they were stoned in American History. Occasionally Dwayne stopped the car and leaned out the window to fire at a high circling hawk or a jetliner rumbling from coast to coast.

The afternoon deepened and the humidity created a dreamy haze that obscured the clarity of distant buildings and treelines. The clear line of the horizon melted away like dirty snow. They turned off the gravel road onto the parallel ruts that led down to the river, past a charred foundation of a gutted house and the blackened trunk of a cottonwood snag that was slick and glossy. A grasshopper whirred through an open window, clung to the dash before Dwayne grabbed it, crushed it in his palm, then threw it out the window. Tall cheat grass slapped against the underside of the car.

The music, at high volume, flashed through the car, eroding the silence at the edges but paradoxically deepening the silence within. It was there, deep inside that silence, on the way to the river, that Craig tried to imagine a man's death. But images from a screen kept intruding—a television or movie image of a shot heard from another room, beyond a door, the sound of a collapsing body, then the stupid terror on the face of a relative or lover. He couldn't get to the heart of that silence. Some black specks that must have been crows flared across the sky. If they called, the boys could not hear them.

The road ended at the river, at the edge of a plowed field where the water had carved a large notch into the field. Each year more and more of the field had fallen into the river even though the notch was filled with a world of debris: black, tread-bare tires, stripped car bodies and rust-eaten pickup beds, shattered storm doors and window frames, splintered lumber and coils of barbwire, outdated refrigerators and stoves and broken chairs and torn couches and shattered televisions. Everything, even the television sets, had been riddled with gunshots.

Craig leaned against the car, listening to the Doors, while Dwayne fired down into the debris, ripping holes in rusty fenders, flipping aluminum cans into the air, shattering glass where he could find it. A rat scurried over a hubcap and found cover in a milk carton imprinted with the image of a lost child. Dwayne's shot glanced off the hubcap.

When he grew bored he wandered along the riverbank. The bank was steep, and the brown water was swift and topped with a milky froth. The silver belly of a dead carp floating by caught the glint of the sun. Dwayne fired at a cottonwood snag, then at some dark logs under an overhanging willow. It might have been a raft; it was hard to tell. After the second shot a skinny, ragged boy rose up from the river brush like a ghost from the past. He flipped a muddy finger at the sky and yelled up at Dwayne to go to hell.

When Dwayne snapped the bolt on his .22 the boy dove back into the brush.

"Hell, I wasn't goin' to kill the little river rat," he said, as if Craig were beside him. "I just wanted to put the fear of God into him. That's all."

Craig heard the shots as part of the gathering thunder of "Riders on the Storm." The over-under sagged in the crook of his arm as his fingers drummed along with the rising storm . . . *into this house we're born* . . . as the image of an uncle he never knew, an Uncle Will, formed and dissolved as a burst of fire broke across his chest at the thought of the girl last night and then he remembered that his aunt had once said he had beautiful hands. It was as close as he could get to his uncle.

When Dwayne returned they began to wander across the plowed field toward the surrounding grove of cottonwoods. A breeze they could not feel stirred the top of the cottonwoods and shook loose the white angel floss that settled like snow on their shoulders and in their hair. Craig tried to imagine a meadow flush with prairie hens, turkeys, deer, antelope, and perhaps a herd of bison filing down to the river. His forearm burned from the friction of the gun. It was a heavy gun. Heavy for a tired man to lift up to his own head or chest or whatever. The barrel banged against his shins as he stumbled over a thick slab of soil and stubble. Dwayne had said that behind the ear was the best place, but the image of a forlorn man in a darkened cellar kneeling over a gun as if in prayer had etched itself in his mind with all the authority of a fact, but he couldn't reconcile that dark figure with the aunt who had said he had beautiful hands. The link between them was like the fine wire in a fence line that disappeared into the horizon. Silence filled the space between them, between his aunt and uncle, his mother and father. There was silence within the sighs of the girl, even between his buddy Dwayne and him. It was weird—scary and sacred.

The coyote that emerged from the grove saw them before they saw it. It skirted the field, emerging from the dried weeds, floating sideways it seemed, its quick, thin legs churning under a body thick as a log. Its bushy tail was long enough to sweep its tracks. Stopping, it sniffed the ground, stole a longer inquisitive look at the strange figures stumbling across the familiar field, then sniffed the air, panted, and seemed to find the boys unworthy of serious attention.

When Dwayne saw it he stopped and grabbed Craig's arm. "Shh!" he hissed, pointing across the field and dropping to his knees.

The coyote glanced up, then returned to the scent of a field mouse as the boys held their breath.

A cloud passed over the sun and swathed the field in shadow. The high silver leaves in the trees rattled and then the sun burst from the cloud. Craig felt sweat oozing from above his lips; his forehead glittered like the leaves on the tree.

The coyote looked up from its scented trail, cocked its head to catch a sound or scent that rode the breeze. It may have been the squeal of its pups, a mate's call, the boy's new scent, or something unknown in the wind itself.

"Take 'im!" Dwayne whispered. "You can get 'im with the .410."

Dwayne's voice came from beyond the pale, from beyond the door, prodding and dependent as Craig, kneeling, raised the gun to his shoulder, sighted down the dark barrel as if peering into a tunnel. At the end of the barrel the coyote panted, gazed at the boys, nipped at its flank, then cocked its head to catch a sound or scent in the breeze before flattening itself against the ground as if coiled for ambush or a dance.

The safety was off, and Craig's finger was curled around the trigger as the moment deepened and widened and the door opened to images of an unknown relative hunched in prayerful despair and an aunt who observed beautiful hands, the empty houses and all the something or other places along the way, gutted churches, forgotten cemeteries, the world of debris and the river and his parents adversarial wounds and the girl's warm breath and refusal—the sacred space and silence between them. Sweat burst from his brow, beaded and ran down into his eyes. He felt as if he was about to shout at someone in prayer, profane the inner sanctum of a church, pry open the heart of the girl he was with last night.

"Christ, take 'im!" Dwayne hissed. "He's yours!"

The coyote leapt to its feet, sashayed, snapped at something in the air, and then keened in the breeze. A shower of white floss fell from the cottonwoods, clung to the coyote's pelt and began drifting toward the boys like a unifying snow.

In the lingering hush Dwayne waited and waited, his breath tightening until he saw the gun barrel drop and a strange, serene expression on his friend's face.

"What the fuck is goin' on?" He grabbed for the gun.

But it wouldn't come free as he pulled and twisted until the two of them fell into a stubbled furrow and began rolling over and over as their legs churned for a purchase. Sweat that had started on their brows ran down their cheeks, burst from their forearms, broke in a line across their shoulders and coursed down their backs. Their shirts tore and jeans ripped at the knees.

Dwayne wrestled for leverage, for possession of the gun that had disappeared between them as Craig's hands circled the barrel and the stock, not because he wanted it or was afraid to lose it, but because it was part of him now, a legacy beyond possession or surrender. He'd restored it. His hands were hinges to a door that was blowing in the wind, as the two of them wrestled like mythic twins warring in the womb.

The coyote, puzzled and curious, tilted its head, whined and pawed at the ground.

It didn't spook at the sudden burst of noise, like the crack of lightning before rain; instead it crouched and peered along the ground as one of the thunder-makers across the field collapsed like settling dust while the other rose up, roared, and kicked dirt on the quiet, fallen one who seemed already to be melting into the ground like the last snow.

The scent of a strange, fresh blood reached the coyote. The blood made it wary. It rose on quick legs, sniffed the air, found a familiar scent that came up from the river, then loped along the edge of the field, back into the grove to feed its young.

# A Strange Deal

*They were one of those families who came and went a lot, the kind it's tough to get a line on, a family without beginnings. They lived in a trailer outside of town or rented an old house that needed paint and shingles. The father hired on driving truck during harvest or filled orders at the co-op, and with all the other boys in the family, it was hard to get a fix on the one, David, who came back into town in a coffin draped with a flag.*

*It was David, not Daniel, his brother, who was unfit. It was David. Not Daniel.*

*David.*

*He never played football or basketball or dated anyone special; there were just some vague memories of him fishing the river down by the Armsted place and cruisin' Main on Saturday night with the Perkins boy in that green Impala that always glittered like a mirage; most folks, in fact, probably weren't even aware that he left town, had gone anywhere special at all.*

*At the funeral the preacher, the one before Newhart came to town, ol' Hartman, wasn't even sure, exactly, where the boy had been. He had to look it up, and then he wasn't sure, exactly, how to say it. In his sermon he just called it another world.* It was a tragic death in another world, *he said. That's what he said.*

*It was a beautiful fall day. In the country the combines whirled through the fields of brown sorghum, crows beckoned and taunted as they fled over the crimson hedgerows, pheasants skittered along the edge of cornfields, and in town folks raked up leaves, cleaned their storm windows as the liquid voice on the radio pitched and rolled with the fortunes of a game.*

*At the cemetery, the stoic veterans of other wars, wrapped in their starched uniforms, fired a salute into the deep azure sky, and as they walked away, after the coffin was lowered into the ground, they were shaking their heads and loosening their brass buttons.*

It's a strange deal, *one of them said.* A strange kind of deal.

# When the Blood Came Faster than the Water

Even from the warmth of his bed in winter, his gaze moves in a slow serpentine march as he visits and revisits the scene: out from the frosted window to the forked branches of the apple tree in the yard, then beyond to the desolate brown fields and hedgerows of gnarled and twining branches like razor wire, up to that cold distant star in the north, then back down to the burnished hills around Turk's Bluff where the sliver of moon is like the light behind a closed door.

There, in memory, a small frame of light opens on a platoon of soldiers scattered like a handful of dice on an ashen hillside.

Some of the soldiers lean against charred stumps or splintered logs, softly drumming their fingers against their weapons or blowing ash from the clip as if blowing hair from a girl's brow.

Others sprawl on their backs against the seared slope of a crater or hunch forward over small cans of food, a cigarette, or the charity of letters. All of them have taken on the charred color of the land.

A boy rolls a smooth marble in his palms then pulls a comic book from his pack. Another boy, with curly red hair, rests his freckled cheek on his arched knee as he traces a sooty finger over a glossy photo of a teenage girl unfathomably clean and safe.

Beside him, leaning against the same blackened stump, Dietz flips a shriveled, blackened ear in the air, calling heads or tails. *Heads we live, tails we die,* he says, lifting his charred hand, laughing at the gamble.

Over time, in the hands of the jaded and weary, the ear has transcended perversity to a place of reverence and devotion. It has a name, Uncle Charley, and whoever walks point or feels acutely unlucky is designated the keeper of the ear. Sometimes they confess to it as if it were a priest, confide their deadliest sins, their fear, and beseech it for absolution.

*Two out of three,* Dietz laughs, flipping it again.

From the warm bedroom, viewed from a distance, the scene holds a grotesque beauty for Gil—out there in the brown hills under the North Star, so far away. The scene of the soldiers at rest on the ravaged hillside, cooled by their sweat glistening on their sooty, smudged faces, savoring for a moment the serenity of fatigue and their macabre talisman under a powder sky. A stay in the battle for hearts and minds.

The bed creaks as he draws his knees up closer to his chest, settles the covers around his shoulders. On the other side of the bed Shirley's sleep is seductive—a dream unfathomably distant, like the girl in the glossy photo. The comforter over her shoulders rises and falls with her breath, its blue folds are like the contours of a dune in the valley between them. The scent of flannel sheets, warm flesh, lotion and shampoo linger over the dunes. In sleep, in comfort, her slow breath is as rhythmic as the tides. His own aches in his throat as he stares out at the hillside under the sliver of moon.

Out there, in that place, he believes, he can fix the memory, chain it like a dog. Then he can sleep.

But inevitably there is the descent. Always the descent. And one by one, the charred men under the North Star begin to disappear through a hole in the earth, as if they are sliding down the sides of a funnel.

First there is Dietz, the keeper of the ear, who volunteers, and then the boy with the marble, too dazed and awed to be frightened; and then the boy with the glossy photo, who knew his fate and so passed the picture along to Gil, and then another and another—Caps, Retch, Chicken—boys christened with absurd names to separate them from themselves. One by one they all entered the tunnel.

And Gil, a witness even then, waited as a fly buzzed around his face and a mosquito tried to pierce the layers of dust and soot on his neck.

Down in the lowlands of tropical firs and coconut trees, the steam was rising and the jungle canopy was pocked with charred holes. Out of the mist and foliage strange birds called, and in the north a column of smoke and red dust rose like a pillar in the dreamy netherlands.

The charred hill had been claimed before, and the tunnel had been cleared before. Again and again they'd pitched down grenades, emptied mags of M-16s, waited for the smoke and dust to clear then entered the abyss.

Once, last winter, in the Greener Pasture, the Spook, in his corner by the jukebox, told Gil what it was like.

He'd gone down, he said.

He'd been there.

*It was a fuckin' maze,* he said. *A maze.*

They drank beer, and Spook clutched the can with both hands as he stared out at the dance floor, at the remote, sinuous courtship of dancers reeling under the blue light.

*There was a ladder,* Spook said. *Bamboo.* It rattled against the stone as he descended, and the little circle of blue sky kept shrinking and shrinking until he stepped into a small pool of water at the bottom.

In the darkness, all he had to go on, he said, were his hands. *The hands don't lie,* he said. *What you see or smell or hear or taste can trick you, but the hands don't lie,* he said.

His own breath echoed in the tunnel. The water splashed against the slick sides as he groped along the wall until he found an opening on his right, ducked into it because it was all that there was, followed it into a deeper darkness that funneled down until he had to crouch, duck-walk, then finally crawl. The floor was smooth and slick and the rats were fearless. The fur of one grazed his cheek and its quick claws pricked the flesh on his shoulder then down his back and legs as it scurried away. *It knew where it was goin',* Spook said. *It wasn't lost.*

*There was an ol' boy from back east who found the light at the end of the tunnel,* Spook said, a thin slice of light at the end of the tunnel, so he'd bellied up closer, smeared mud on any part of him that was still white and tried to breathe through his skin as he leveled the .45 at the thin light behind a veil and was about to fire off a round when the veil rose and the full light burst into the tunnel. He heard a clamor of voices and the rattling of tin, smelled rice and a damp body scent as he fired into the voices and the light. The smell of powder filled the tunnel as gunshots exploded, ricocheted, and screeched against the walls.

The echo was deafening, bouncing from wall to wall long after the men in the lighted room beyond the veil had vanished and the blood was trickling from his throat. He cupped his ears rather than his throat and when they hauled him up, they said he looked like one of those hear-no-evil monkeys, and the whole time blood was oozing from his throat. *He shouldn't of looked up,* Spook said.

*He shouldn't of looked up at the light. Me, I never saw no light,* Spook said. *I just crawled around in circles. In the dark. Ended up comin' out where I went in. Didn't even have a wound to show for it. Just a helluva lot of fear.*

I saw 'em come up, Gil said. I saw Deitz come up. At first I thought he was bloated, swollen with purple mud. He was panting, and his eyes were wild and white, and then I realized it wasn't just him.

There were two of 'em, almost. There was another head and other arms and a torso wrapped up against his chest; we had to pry them apart. It was the curly, red-haired kid, clinging to Deitz like the devil, and it wasn't until we pried them apart and lay him down we could see it was just the top half of 'im because where his legs should a been, there was only shreds of bloodied cloth dangling like some giant scythe had come along and clipped him clean, except it wasn't clean.

Doc stuck 'im with morphine and we knelt over 'im and poured water from our canteens over his face and shoulders, trying to flush away the blood and ash and mud, but the blood came faster than the water and pooled in a purple stain on the ground while Deitz, crazed, pent-up, circled the tunnel like a yelping dog, cursed and fired down into the darkness. All that came back was his own echo.

Then Deitz came over to the kid, and I thought he was goin' to yell at him or kick him, but instead he bent over, lifted 'im up in his two arms, bore him up in the cradle of his arms, and staggered down the hillside, away from the tunnel and the tight circle of men, and there, fifteen yards away, down by a charred log, he laid him down.

He knelt over 'im and pointed with his left hand down into the valley, to the green canopy and the mist and the rising birds while the pistol in his right hand rose from his hip, leveling near the kid's ear and there was a soft whimper, not of fear but more of relief, and then the quick crack, like the splintering of a branch, and the kid's arms jerked, his hands fell and opened as his chest rose and fell, and there was only the thinnest trickle of fresh blood because he had already given it all up.

Deitz lay an open hand on his chest, lingered for a moment, then slowly rose stoop-shouldered, quieted now himself, and shuffled back up the hill, on past us, farther up the hill, to his pack, where he sat alone eating a can of peaches as he gazed down into the valley.

*It was a gift, I figure,* Gil told Spook. *It was the only gift he knew how to give.* He was that kind of guy. It was that kind of place. I dropped the picture of the girl down the tunnel. There was no name on it, nothin'. She may have been a fantasy. A lot of guys did that, carried pictures of a fantasy, to make them feel better. I had to empty my hands, Gil said. Spook nodded. He understood.

From the bedroom window the moon has vanished from the frame of the frosted window. In the encroaching darkness, the apple tree and hedgerows and burnished hills have faded away. Even the North Star is gone.

Now, if he can find a place to rest his hands, he can sleep. . . . Turning, he stares into the web of Shirley's brown hair fanned across the pillow, a fragile, pink ear looks like a crescent moon through a crease in her hair. Her thin, white fingers curl into her palms in front of her face on the pillow as if she fell asleep anticipating a prayer.

There is no place for his own hands in bed. He reaches out to rest a hand on her hip, but the distance between them is too great, so he allows it to settle in the space between them, in the valley of the comforter.

They feel alien to him, his own hands, heavy and empty and cold. Until he finds a place for them, it will be hard to sleep.

# Show Business

*On Wednesday nights ol' Cheat would hay his cattle early, go in and shower and rub a little Aqua Velva on his cheeks; and then after letting his wife off at the church basement for her Ladies' Auxiliary meeting, he would slip away to the Greener Pasture.*

*At 9:15 Marge had three fingers of Old Crow waiting, and Cheat would take a hitch on his trousers, slide onto his stool at the center of the bar, and commence with his stories, ceasing only at five minutes to eleven, when he would pop a wintergreen Lifesaver in his mouth and retreat home, by way of the church basement.*

*In his seventy-eight years there was nothing he hadn't seen.*

*He'd seen the huge piles of buffalo hides and bleached skulls and bones beside the railroad tracks, Custer himself leading that doomed blue column across the plains up toward the Dakotas as the strains of Gerry Owens and the clomp of hooves and creak of artillery faded in the wind.*

*He'd seen the great Sioux warrior Touch the Clouds racing his pony on a northern bluff, played cards with Wyatt Earp, Bat Masterson, and could vouch that Wild Bill Hickok always took the whiskey bottle in his left hand so as to keep his gun hand free.*

*He'd spent a night in a cyclone shelter with Calamity Jane (a rough ol' gal, Cheat said), and when the buffalo dried up, he'd advised William Cody to consider show business because that's where the future was for someone who was ambitious and willing to forgo his name.*

*It was to Cheat's place that Jesse James came in drag, seeking refuge* (a prettier gal than ol' Calamity, if you ask my opinion, *Cheat said) and then there was John Brown with that Old Testament fire burning in those righteous eyes. Cheat was a witness as Brown compelled a slaveholder to bow and pray for his immortal soul before slaughtering 'im then and there like a fat hog.*

*He'd seen children playing with a corpse of a hanged man like a tether ball, and it had been his own mother who drove away some straggling Indians from the door of her soddy by brandishing a picture of the Crucifixion.*

*He'd concealed runaway slaves in his potato cellar, guided the Exodusters on their pilgrimage to the Promised Land, and helped that kid down south, Walter Johnson, with his aim when he saw him chucking stones at squirrels. He offered up a few pointers on tactics and weapons to that boy Ike when they played soldier down by the creek, and even told that Hughes boy to leave this silent land and go back East and practice on his verse; by God, he sure enough did, and then there were the blizzards of '84, the flood of '52, the scriptural plagues of locusts and dust, and once he'd even taken a whetstone to Carrie Nation's ax. Yes sir. Ya' betcha!*

Put a good edge on it, *he said,* even though I didn't much agree with her ways.

Ol' Cheat, he's something else, *they'd say when he'd left.* He oughta write a book, or be in show business. There's pretty good money to be made in lyin'.

# The Greener Pasture

"Ol Marge there wore me out," Sonny said, lifting a leg to slide onto the stool and then raising the chaser Marge had promised as a reward for the dance.

Beside him Slug, intransigent as a tree stump, was swirling his beer and wondering without malice what the hell the world was coming to. On the TV, above the rows of dark bottles, some cheerleaders from Memphis cartwheeled across a stage, then mounted one another's shoulders, smiled, and tossed their heads like horses, snapping their ponytails in unison, before the pyramid collapsed into a dramatic kaleidoscope of tumbles and somersaults—and still they smiled.

"Memphis," Slug was saying as if trying to retrieve a dream. "You ever been to Graceland?"

"I knew this gal once," Sonny said. "She smelled like fresh rain. She treated me like a god. I'd forgotten about her."

It was the dance that had brought her back. The dance and the Coors and the chaser and the Greener Pasture brought up a lot of things. She had these tiny breasts, like raindrops, and they glittered above him in the gray light of a small room in San Francisco as a streetcar clattered outside. In his palms he could still feel them, soft and warm as a horse's nose, but he didn't tell Slug that, a man didn't tell those kinds of things.

In the Greener Pasture a man could still dream. As the world outside darkened, pitched deeper into midnight, the voices inside would quicken, hands would erupt in search of a shoulder or settle on a forearm or tease across a thigh; there would be the quick easy joke, the rattle of pool balls—and then there was the music, always the music to carry the dreamer into those wide horizons. Sometimes it was all a man had, Sonny thought, till the weather warmed and the fish would take a lure.

There was that night, not too long ago, when Sonny and the boys—Leon and Vic and Leo—had smoked big cigars, leaned back in their chairs, put their boots on the table as they floated down that river of beer and bumps, they called it, rolling with the current of the music and the swell of voices and the glad-hand laughter, swaggering with Bob Wills and *Big Balls in Cowtown*—his runnin' buddies, Leon and Vic and Leo—the Wheeler-Dealers they called themselves, searching for the right nasal pitch as the scent of clover drifted in from the field across the road and a ball game on the TV lingered across time like an image on an old urn—the wheeler-dealers full of themselves, jawing at first about trading pickups for new rigs with air and power and the whole shit-and-caboodle loaded works and then gobblin' up a little land where oil oozed out of the ground like a good head on a beer. They bought pork bellies, hedged wheat and soybeans, wheeled and dealed in futures, conspired takeovers, leveraged buyouts and thrived on estates with white fences and arches over the driveway as majestic as the goddamned pearly gates themselves.

By midnight, herds of Arabians grazed in their pastures, peacocks strutted in their backyards, and Leo, red-eyed and laughing before he fell off his chair, had a wife as sweet as Dolly Parton who wore one of those flimsy teddy-deals when she curled up on the couch with 'im to watch Monday night football.

Then Marge, patient behind the bar, watching the clock, keeping the tab while they imagined their fortunes, chased them back out into the night where the dog-day cicadas were sassy and mocking, and Sonny, missing his house on the first try, circled the block; and when he finally found his way into bed, his wife's pale, sloping back looked like a remote, polished stone. It was a stone he dared not disturb.

"She treated me like a god," he said, curling his fingers into his empty palms. But Slug was still trolling his memories of Memphis. He rubbed his stubbed finger against his cheek. The flesh on the end was taunt and creased, like the corner of a fitted sheet. The tip of it, long ago, had fallen down an oil well in Oklahoma. Somewhere in the panhandle.

"I went through there once. In that '67 Coupe de Ville I had. Paid $500 for it. Had a piece of bailing wire to hold down the hood, but she did alright. I never made it to Graceland, though."

Marge slid another bottle of Coors in Sonny's direction, then peeled a bill from the loose change on the bar.

"Seen the boys?" Sonny asked.

Marge winked, then shook her head. "Not in a month of Sundays. Leon took a job in Wichita, I heard. Overhaulin' computers or somethin', I don't know. Vic's ex-wife came to town, I guess, all dressed up in a suit." She squeezed Sonny's hand in a way that confused him. When they'd danced he'd taken her hand like the handle of a saw and pushed and pulled like a man cutting through green wood before settling into a slow dance.

He'd dipped to the side, scooted forward, dipped to the other side, leaned into her and dropped his cheek down into the cushion of her hair as he hummed and then crooned along with Bob Wills and the Texas Playboys as they rose on the pinched, desperate wings of *Faded Love,* rising and rising, clinging to the wings of those sweet, taut fiddles—so achingly sweet and maudlin and earnest that they finally burst through the bubble of their own sentiment and emerged on the other side into a sublime winter light.

He'd swooned, pressed closer to Marge. Leaning into her, he longed for the scent of rain. He edged his hand and hers in closer to their bodies, then between their bodies, between his chest and hers, in tight; then slowly his fingers uncurled, opening like the mouth of a fish blindly bottom-feeding along the buttons of her blouse until his thumb found a pucker, a gap between the buttons, and with visions of raindrops and the velvet nose of a horse in his palm, he crooned, *like heaven would miss the stars above,* rising on those wings of longing until abruptly she reversed the grip, grabbed his hand, squeezed it like a dishrag, and hung it out to dry.

She bit his neck and hissed in his ear. "Just dance cowboy. Leave the milkin' for the barn."

"Oh, hell, Marge, what's a little feel between friends," Sonny had whined.

"You wouldn't want it in the light of day," Marge said.

Now, at the bar, she squeezed his hand again. "You get carried away, hon. That's your problem. That's the horse bitin' back. What feels good will up and bite ya. You oughta know that."

"Hells bells," Sonny said, shaking his head. "What a man don't come in for."

"Dry holes," Slug said. "Dry holes. That's what a man comes in for."

But Sonny was looking up at the TV, at a Chevy truck bouncing over a field of stone. It gave him hope.

Behind them the dance floor was empty. Blue-gray smoke rose from the tables and drifted up toward the light. At the pool table Leonard and Willard, their flesh and clothes covered by the white silt of the co-op, kept circling the constellations of spheres, intent on angles and the chain of connections on the green felt. A pretty blue cloud was trapped under the Coors' chandelier.

In a booth against the far wall, a short wiry man and a round, fleshy woman leaned into the darkened corner as their hands groped under the table for ecstasy.

"Corner pocket," Leonard said, leaning over the pool table, stroking a kiss off the eight ball then shaking his head and chalking his cue.

At the jukebox, a girl with long blond hair, a girl too beautiful for love, swayed as she watched her reflection in the flashing lights. The lights flickered over her bare, elegant arms and legs. She was barefoot, and her toenails were painted red, and the thin boy beside her had his hands in his pocket and his hat pulled low over his eyes. He looked like some unspeakable terror had turned him to stone.

Beside the jukebox, Gil and Spook hunched forward, nodded as they told their stories of war. Spook's cane hung by the crook on the edge of the scarred table.

The girl at the jukebox shifted her weight from foot to foot, her hair swayed from side to side, uncovering one bare shoulder then the other as her fingers moved over the buttons. Even in the silence her mind was full of melodies.

"Found a taker for your house yet?" Slug asked.

Sonny shook his head, still staring at the Chevy truck bouncing over a field of stone.

"How much you askin'?"

"A fair price," Sonny said. "Enough to satisfy the banker."

"Well, cuttin' your losses ever once in a while ain't no sin," Slug said.

"The work oughta pick up a little in the spring," Sonny said. "Maybe we'll find us a little place out away from town. Buy a double-wide. Start fresh with a garden and some horses."

"A man can always hope for the best," Slug said. "There ain't no law that says he can't."

"The missus ain't too keen on leavin' town, though. Says she'll leave me first."

Slug tapped his finger on his glass as he stared up at the TV. "Worse things could happen," he said. "You oughta set your sights on one of those," he said, nodding at the Chevy pickup bouncing over a field of stone.

"A man could draw on that for a while."

That's what Sonny was thinking. That was something a man could draw on for a while. He could see himself, idling through town with his arm forked out the window. A big antenna on top. A crew-cab with a little chrome to catch the sun. White, or maybe red, if he felt a little cocky. There was something about a man steppin' out of a rig like that that was different. It made him think again of the boys, the wheeler-dealers, and that night when they wheeled and dealed and smoked cigars and sliced up life like a fresh apple pie. But glancing over his shoulder, all he saw were Leonard and Willard, like ghosts circling the pool table, a haze of smoke and obscure shadows in a corner booth, a clamor of voices and glasses, laughter, the girl too beautiful for love and the terrified boy, and Gil and Spook.

Then Spook rose and took up his cane, shoved chairs aside and hobbled across the dance floor and around the pool table.

The cane tapped against the floor as it neared the bar.

"The son of a bitch could walk regular if he wanted to," Slug said. "Hell, anybody who can climb the water tower and take potshots at the goddamned stars can walk if you ask me. That's what I heard, anyway."

Spook hobbled past the bar toward the hallway and then the girl too beautiful for love finally made her choice, Martha and the Vandellas, and it all began again—out of the corners the dancers emerged in quest of the green light. They sought one another's hands and eyes as they merged, parted, and swayed. They sang or mouthed the words, taunted their partners with teasing fingers. A scent of flesh and sweat and a sweet defiance filled the room. The floor vibrated and glasses rattled on the tables. They teased. Their arms rose and opened above their bobbing heads and shoulders, reaching up toward the smokey green light as if beckoning the deity to come on down, get funky with us, and dance with us in the murky light and sweaty flesh of the Greener Pasture . . . *There's no place to run, no place to hide.*

It was good again, and Sonny, his mind on a new rig, put a hand on Slug's shoulder and rose from his bar stool, stepped back, staggered, grabbed the bar for support as if it were the side of a boat, then smiled boyishly and remembered his intention.

"Nature's callin'," he said. "Got to water the horses." Gazing across the dance floor was like staring into a fire, and there was no mystery to why flames were said to dance. He listed toward those flames, a flush came to his cheeks, and something frozen hard inside, behind his eyes, was melting like butter. He remembered nature's call, the horses he was obligated to water, and concentrated on the walk ahead of him, around the bar to the hallway and the plywood door with *Stallions* burned into the wood.

It was dark in the hallway and the splintered floor sagged, then seemed to roll underfoot. The *Stallions* door was locked, so he leaned against the wall, beside a pay phone, where hundreds of numbers and names had been scribbled or carved into the wood. Out of a dull remembrance he dropped a coin in the phone and beseeched a hollow voice to connect him to the girl who smelled like fresh rain, whose breasts were like rain drops, but he was at a loss to provide a name or number as letters—K, L, M, H, F—fell from the alphabet and finally into a whir of what sounded like a locust he mumbled, *she treated me like a god.*

Then there was a clamor of porcelain and steel, a rush of water, and the *Stallions* door opened, and Spook's head and shoulders leaned over a cane before he shuffled out into the hallway. Sonny pressed back against the wall to let him pass.

But Spook stopped, straightened over his cane. He smelled of smoke and stale beer and pork rinds. His eyes appeared suddenly like fireflies in the darkened hallway. He smiled at Sonny.

"Makin' any money?" he asked.

*I got a deal goin'*, Sonny tried to say, but the words caught in his throat like a death rattle. By the time he'd swallowed and tried again, Spook had turned, leaned back over his cane and was hobbling back out into the bar.

Sonny's hand leapt out, as if swiping at the two elusive fireflies, but it was a swipe into the darkness and thin air and propelled him against the door that said *Mares.* A voice from inside scolded and commanded patience as Sonny righted himself, rocked on his heels, then sought a stance that would carry him through the night.

The door that led outside was open, and he could see the cars and trucks in the parking lot, the passing headlights on the highway, the neon lights of a convenience store across the way. A couple, giggling and disheveled, brushed past him, drawn by the green light of the dance floor and the music that ebbed out into the night. Sonny wondered if she had breasts like raindrops, but the thought vanished as quickly as the fireflies.

He went on out the door, humming *Faded Love* as he groped his way through the maze of cars and trucks in the parking lot. The steel was cold to the touch, and the gravel underfoot sounded like glass breaking into tiny pieces.

The green-yellow, pulsing lights of the Greener Pasture, the sassy laughter and teasing, reckless voices bouncing on the waves of the music all began to recede into the wide horizon of the west. It all sounded like distant tribal voices vanishing into the past as he rolled along through the labyrinth of steel and chrome.

At the edge of the parking lot he stopped, leaned against the rusted fender of an old truck. *Like heaven would miss the stars above,* he sang, softly, into the dry night air as he squinted, looking up, above the hazy lights of Paradise. The stars were dull, murky, as if each year they, too, were receding. In his memory they were brighter than that, formed from a solid sheet of light struck with a hammer. He'd always thought of God, in the beginning, with a sledgehammer, bringing it down on a solid sheet of light, the shards becoming stars and God growling, *there, there you sons a bitches, there's your light for the night.*

Sonny felt the ache in his bladder and remembered nature's call.

He fumbled with his zipper, with his shirttail and underwear in a struggle to find himself. *Patience, patience,* he muttered, digging himself out, until he was again looking up at the sky. The longer he looked and the lighter he felt, the brighter the stars became, and soon he was singing, *it was in the spring time* and thinking about that Chevy truck he'd seen and that maybe he'd go back inside the Greener Pasture for another round and dance with Marge. The night was young.

He thought he smelled fresh rain in the night air. Rain drops. Hell, it was hard to imagine a man who wouldn't look at the stars while he pissed. It was just human nature.

# A Useless Pile of Rocks

*From her room in the home Aggie stares across a plowed field at the coarse leaves of a surviving sunflower, drooping under the unbearable weight of its own seed—and then beyond, to the untillable border where the once taunt, shiny barbwire fence that long ago snatched a piece of her skirt now sags brittle and rusty in the thick prairie grass—and then further, up the hill, further than she can see, in memory now, she wanders the ancient path up the south slope to the clearing, spreading a quilt, matting the sparse grass within the circle of sandstone at the top of Turk's Bluff.*

*She remembers when Buck fenced it off, seven years into their marriage. When he separated the good land from the useless pile of rocks, he called it, a useless pile of rocks that had been in the family longer than anyone could remember. A useless pile of rocks he called it again and again. Untillable. So he fenced it off, separated it from the good land, strung barbwire up at the base of the hill like the dividing line between a heaven and hell turned upside down, and so the hill became a forbidden land, forgotten, swept from the collective memory.*

*Then one day Will-Jonah appeared as if spawned by the useless pile of rocks or dropped by a circling hawk as rejected prey.*

*But Buck never run him off because he was just a useless pile of bones on a useless pile of rocks—his exact words, Aggie remembers—and then for seven barren years she would stand before the kitchen window, lean on the sink and gaze through the thick summer heat that tore asunder every tree, post, and rooftop, filtered the landscape through a dream, turned roads into rivers and spread shimmering pools over the hard-scrabble yard.*

*And then the sultry night when Buck was gone (in pursuit of happiness), she left the airless house in search of the breeze, the windsickness and open spaces that had terrified her mother and grandmother, slid through the barbed fence, snagging her dress before she could gather it against her thighs, then wandered barefoot up the slope of Turk's Bluff until her hair blew into the corner of her mouth and her dress fluttered and snapped like a flag. From the east the wedge of a train light pried through the valley floor, opening the night along the suture of tracks. In the wake of the train some clouds burst into relief behind a spasm of lightning.*

*She had mounted the crest when his voice came out of the darkness. The first words of the night. The first words in years, it seemed. "We need the rain," Will-Jonah said, and no more did she hear the words than she felt the first heavy drops against her flesh as if the words themselves were water.*

*On the grassy spot within the circle of stone, surrounded by sumac and soapwood, they watched the crackling sheets of lightning burst across the brutal sky, and when the rain, hard, slanted in, he leaned over her, shielding her from the sting, and in the storm her quick breath mingled inseparably with his as the water dripped through his beard, coursed down her cheek and shimmered like a mirage on her breasts.*

*So henceforth in Buck's absence she climbed the hill in darkness on the swathed trail and retreated into the kitchen by daybreak. And Buck knew, she thought, he must have known even though he did not know, and when he left without leaving as a man will do, he must have seen in the boy she named Junior the useless pile of bones destined for a useless pile of rocks. Even a man like Buck must know a little of what she knew. Even a man like Buck must know that Junior was not his, she was not his, nothing on the whole wide earth was truly his.*

# The Visitation

*He's got to be apprehended,* Digger was saying. *There's a law! You just can't go buryin' folks where ever you damn well please. Irregardless.* He pressed close to the sheriff, peered up into the shadowy crack between the brim of the sheriff's hat and thick shoulders. The sheriff rocked back and forth as his thumb plied the slit between his wide belt and stomach. They stood beside the empty white hearse, on main street, and already a crowd was gathering around them, watching them, watching the sky, watching the purple shadows of the evening gather over Turk's Bluff. The news was spreading.

In the beginning it sounded like the encroaching hum of locusts, then a stirring in the air that rattled the brittle leaves of the elms like old bones. The first whispers and mutterings escaped the closed homes and air-conditioned offices and hummed through the telephone lines. At the M & P Cafe fresh peach pie and hot coffee were abandoned on the counter, at the Greener Pasture cold beer and chasers were left on the bar, on the kitchen tables homegrown tomatoes and sweet corn soaked into paper plates; and even in dens and family rooms, the spasmodic light of television sets illuminated empty recliners and couches as house-coated women with curlers in their hair and fish-bellied men in floral shorts barefooted their way to the curb, glanced up and down the street, searching for neighbors to confirm the news.

Under the ornamental maples and plums, children who had been turning somersaults and awaiting the appearance of fireflies sprawled in the grass and plucked three-leaf clovers as they peered up at the strangeness of the world they were destined to enter.

It was late in August, when the evenings usually slipped with the sun into a quiet, humid placidity so deep that the town of Paradise itself seemed to vanish under the tall elms.

But now the townspeople were aroused. They funneled into the heart of town, bunching up like cattle on the sidewalk outside the sheriff's office, between the Rexall Store and Carl's Accounting Service. The news had spread to the countryside, and soon men in overalls, the hair on their arms matted with field dust and alfalfa leaves, leaned against the fenders of their trucks on the edge of the crowd, their eyes on the ground as they shook their heads, toed pebbles on the street, pushed them a little to one side and then the other, then rolled them under the soles of their cracked boots.

*There's no tellin' what a man will do,* one of the men said as he spit, and the others nodded.

*What we don't come in for,* his wife said to the other wives who had formed their own society in front of Irene's Fabric Shop.

Then a hand, man or woman's, rose from the crowd, pointed up to the hills in the northwest where the sky had flared into marbled orange and crimson layers, toward the hill they called Turk's Bluff without knowing why; and two hundred people strained, squinted until they believed they could see him, the one they called Junior without knowing why, a blemish on the radiant southeast slope, hunched under his macabre burden amidst the dark squat stubble of shrubs and sandstone, rising then receding like some vague anomalous protracted pulse.

*In extremis* they found their voices:

*It's the goddamnedest thing I ever heard of,* a man said.

*He just walked right in and took it. That's what I heard.*

*Digger's fit to be tied.*

*Casket and all?*

*The whole kit and caboodle.*

*He just marched right in.*

*Didn't say a damn word?*

*It's the goddamnedest deal I ever heard of.*

*He can't or won't.*

*I think he damn well could if he wanted to.*

*Just took it?*

*It's a strange kind of deal if you ask me.*

*Not a word?*

*A man would have to be a few sheets to the wind to pull a deal like that.*

*A bubble or two off plumb anyhow.*

*Just took it? Didn't say a word?*

*It just goes to show what can happen.*

*Hell, it's been twenty years since he's been back.*

*You can lose your bearings, alright.*

*I don't believe he visited her once in the Nursing Home.*

*Not once in five years.*

*Has it been that long?*

*She went in the same time that Kathryn did.*

*I was thinking it was four.*

*I'm sure it's five.*

*That's right, it was three years ago they sold out when that wild horse caused such a commotion. The same year Sam had his bypass.*

*I wouldn't want to be the one to say it, but if you ask me she was a little on the peculiar side.*

*I will say her chicken gravy wasn't too bad. She never would say what she done to it.*

*There always was a lot of talk. Even before Buck died.*

*Even so, she deserves a proper burial.*

*I always did wonder about him. If he was quite there.*

*What do you s'pose possessed him? Where did he get the gumption?*

*It's the goddamnedest deal I ever heard of.*

*Not a word?*

*Not a damn word!*

On the edge of the crowd, beside the empty white hearse, Digger still was dressed in his brown suit. His small, white hands flew in the air like pigeons flushed from the shadows. *There's a law,* he told the sheriff again. *The plot is already dug. I got a contract for services rendered. The man's got to be apprehended. You just can't run around plantin' folks wherever you damn well please. There's a law!*

Beside him the Reverend Newhart, still clutching a rolled funeral program, nodded in agreement. *It certainly seems inappropriate,* he said.

The sheriff, holding his own council in the darkness under the brim of his felt Stetson, slowly stepped back and tilted his hat. His face was red and sweaty, and his hand settled on the holster strap fastened over his revolver. His pudgy fingers pried at the flap, snapping it like a rubber band as he, too, finally lifted his eyes to the hills, seeking the specter of the vagabond son carrying his mother to rest on the highest point in the country.

A lone turkey vulture circled the summit like a dark ring around the moon, while above the crowd, white streetlights drew the first desperate moths to stave off the night.

*This sure as hell is a new one on me,* the sheriff said.

## I

Looking back, we should have known. You could see it coming.

Just yesterday, or the day before, Leo saw him with that old scythe in his hands, cutting a swath up the side of the hill like a stairway to heaven, just swinging it back and forth in the second sweetest stroke known to man, just easy as you please across the pasture of the old place, crossing the sagging barbwire fence, then up the slope of Turk's Bluff as dumbly purposeful and nonchalant as a grazing cow, all the way to the top—it was the craziest damn thing, Leo said, and about as pointless a thing as a man could do.

The pendulum of the scythe, Leo said, seemed to just pull him along. He was bent, like a man bucking the wind, and that Cubs baseball cap was pulled low over that lean, washboard face of his. His T-shirt, camouflage or just godforsaken dirty, fluttered in the wind, as if pinned to a clothesline, and in the left rear pocket of his denim jeans was that blue book (*Yin* scrawled across the top) and in his right pocket a tarnished, silver flask (*Yang* scratched with a nail).

*For so wiry a man he had big hands,* Leo said. *Big, strong, good hands.* It was those big hands, even more than the desert ridges of his face that told us what he'd been doing for twenty odd years. They were the hands of makeshift work, random labor, loading and unloading freight, wildcatting, welding, roofin', hayin', drivin' truck, splicin' a few more miles onto the engines of old pickups, the mud of the Mekong Delta; hands that could slide like a shadow between the thighs of fat women who chain-smoked Marlboro lights and dreamed of double-wides and a father for her three children, hands quick and strong enough to hold their own on rowdy nights in bars called The Tumbleweed Inn, The Cactus, Big Al's, The Blank Slate, The Last Chance, and probably a weekend stint or two in the county jail. But Leo was only speculating. He had no way of knowing for sure.

Heaven only knows how he received the news of his mother's death. Some said he was working the wharf in Seattle, others said a welding shop in Durango. Whatever and by what means, he appeared in town on the day Aggie died, driving that old Ford pickup that rattled and belched up smoke like the fires of judgment day.

The first day he was all over the place, up and down the streets of Paradise, at the Greener Pasture and the M & P Cafe, then around the countryside like a lost dog sniffing for a scrap of food. He veered this way and that way with his head tilted askance over his shoulder as if walking a straight line or standing plumb with the world was abhorrent to him or maybe he had just given himself up to the shifting winds. Leo couldn't say for sure.

Someone saw him west of town, kneeling in the rubble of the old Lutheran church, poking through shards of stained glass, holding them up to the sunlight like a prospector, weighing them in his hands, then flipping them into the fallen baptismal. Outside, in the cemetery, he drifted among the headstones and plastic wreaths, past his own father's grave and the plot that awaited his mother without once pausing for a moment of silence except to sit on a granite cross and pull on the flask of *Yang*.

Then he drove the mile lines, past all the old home places, the boarded houses and weathered barns, the collapsed fences and rows of rusty disks and spring tooths and listers, old John Deere tractors that had lost their rubber and sheen—all of it disappearing into green islands of pigweed and sunflowers.

He was spotted down by the river, at the bottom of that cut out on the Newby place, where boys came of age shooting at oil drums, shells of old cars, TVs, couches and refrigerators. He squatted on the bank like a savage, conjuring up fish, maybe, or netting them in memory but it all came to the same thing anyway since there haven't been any fish in that river for years.

He wandered over to the Yake's place, climbed the corral fence, and spent an hour immersed in a whirlwind of dust and manure, sorting for no particular reason that nice bunch of Baldy cows and calves, just playing like a kid in water with no intention whatsoever of swimming anywhere at all.

He climbed a haystack, wandered across a plowed field, kicked at the clods, then disappeared into a field of corn and emerged without so much as an ear in his hand, until, finally, in the evening of the day before the funeral, Farley saw him at the old home place, circling the ground where the house and barn once stood, and that old garage that exploded with mice when they dozed it, toeing at the foundation under the thistles, throwing chips of cement to the wind, and then wandering down to the granary, the only building that remained. The corrugated tin sheets on the roof flapped and screeched in the wind, and the heavy door groaned on its rusty rollers.

Farley, chiseling wheat ground in the south field, watched him pull the big door open just enough to slip inside, into the darkness. Damned if he knew why, Farley said, there was just a bunch of useless junk in there—piles of dry rot lumber and busted tool handles, moldy grain sacks and buckets upon buckets of rusted bolts and piles of oil cans and mouse turds and pigeon shit and odds and ends that no one had claimed when Aggie sold out and went into the home—if not for all the junk, Farley said, the whole damned building would have collapsed long ago. It was the junk that held it up, he swore.

The son of a bitch was in there forever, Farley said. In that darkness, like the belly of a whale, doing who knows what, until he, Farley, finally pulled up the chisel and idled up to the granary, intending, he swore, only to be neighborly and commiserate when Junior emerged with a box of dusty yellow dishes and pots and pans, a recipe box, and the handful of old tools, rusted crescent wrenches, ball peen hammers and busted screwdrivers; loaded them into the back of his truck until he finally came out with that ol' scythe in his hands.

*You're welcome to it all,* Farley said, climbing down from the cab of his tractor, thinking that he could save himself a trip to the dump someday. *It can be pretty tough on a man to lose his very own mother. The only one he's likely to have.*

Junior made easy strokes with that scythe, testing the weight, seeking the rhythm. The curve of the handle was like a snake in his hands. His thin hips and shoulders bent with the scythe, swayed with its pendulous rhythm, like a man dancing with the last woman in the bar, near closing, a man whose pride had yielded to his need. The blade of the scythe swooshed through the air in an easy graceful arc.

The blade clipped the brittle head of a fireweed, already dead from spraying, then sparked against a flat piece of shale.

*That may of belonged to that o' codger up the hill,* Farley said, clenching a piece of wheat stubble between his teeth. *That hermit. The horse-breaker. He made a few trips up and down the hill, I heard. Helped out your mom when your dad was gone. Your mother, by all accounts, returned him some favors.*

A dust devil spun across the chiseled fields like a ghost, skittered across the coarse stalks of cropped alfalfa then vanished across the pasture.

*A nice little breeze today,* Farley said. *Without it a man wouldn't stand a chance.* There was a hitch, almost a stutter, in the grace of the stroke, as if a thought had intruded. Then the scythe slowed, wound down until the blade rested on the ground between Junior's feet.

He leaned on the handle, his chin resting on the dark folds of his hands. He gazed across the pasture, where the dust devil had vanished, across the barbwire fence, up the slope of Turk's Bluff. A half dozen quail flushed from a brown clump of grass and a meadowlark swung low, singing, over a spire of soapweed.

In the heat of the afternoon the horizontal flow of life across the land had ceased, dissolved and rose in vaporous waves. The vertical landmarks of trees, silos, rooftops, the anchors of order, dissembled into pools of dreams, vast silver mirages that shifted and shimmered, and only a few birds called as reminders of the life outside the dream. In the dream, nothing would hold. Nothing endured.

Yet in the silence and slow time of the day, inside the dream, something remained inside of Junior. Something that the scythe, the motion, the exertion, the wanderings of the day from church to cemetery to river had not assuaged. It was palpable. Like the swelling of a seed in the belly.

He stared down at the ground, toed a marble-sized rock, rolled it back and forth under the sole of his boot. When he finally looked up there was something in his eyes that reminded Farley of dry, dusty ground splattered with the first drops of rain. Something poignant and forlorn, desperate, promising, hopeful and needy. Something lost and found at the same time. It came commingled in the scent of dust and water.

Junior inhaled like a man about to free himself from a weight that had fallen across his chest. His thin shoulders rose, and his chest swelled; the veins in his neck rose, pulsed; his face turned red, then a bluish-purple. When his mouth opened, his lips quivered and his jaw locked in place. Then his hands began to shake on the handles of the scythe. The blade rattled against the shale, and his whole body tightened, coiled; sweat burst from his brow, but when his breath finally came, expelled from its wrenching turmoil, it bore no discernable word that Farley could grasp, only a deep guttural rumble mixed with the hot pant of an animal run nearly to death.

*I've never seen a man try harder at anything in his life, to no avail,* Farley said. *It was the damnedest thing.*

Then Junior, pale and shrunken, fixed his gaze on the blade of the scythe glimmering in the sun. He winced, then laughed at his own futility.

*Sh . . . sh . . . sh . . . shit,* he said, looking up at Farley, spitting out the last consonant like a seed, then grinned so that black tooth of his looked like the charred stump of a tree.

He squeezed the grips on the scythe, lifted the blade waist high and for a moment Farley, himself, felt as vulnerable as a dry weed.

But Junior turned away, toward the pasture and the hill, recaptured the work of his hands that in lieu of speech would carry him along in service to the scythe, cutting a swath where his mother had once walked; and it was Farley, left with the rumbling idle of his tractor and the scent of diesel fuel in the air, who felt abruptly uprooted.

The rubber of the tire was hot against his forearm and the tread felt like enormous protruding ribs. He retreated into the cab of the tractor, at a loss for words himself. It's the damnedest thing, he thought. The damnedest thing.

## II

So we shouldn't have been surprised what happened at the visitation. You could see it coming. Looking back, you could see it coming.

In the gathering dusk of his third day in town he appeared, soiled and tragic, in the doorway of the funeral home, still unkempt, as if Sunday clothes were foreign, his eyes like cotton swabs on a wound, and behind him the tailgate of the pickup squared flush against the porch, ready to load.

He looked scraped together, like some makeshift kind of deal, someone said, an odd duck engendered by the silence that lingered at the end of that Requiem deal that Digger plays for affect.

The dozen mourners, mostly from the home, confused about who it was they honored this week, and who had endured fire, wind, flood, dust, locusts, drought, smallpox—stood griefless and stoic in clusters of three or four in their Easter suits and floral dresses as they balanced small pieces of white cake on plastic spoons and tested their memories of yesterday's sweltering high or measured their ailments and surgeries as they once had measured rainfall, bushels of wheat or tablespoons of butter.

It was his boots that they heard. Those old creased boots, bowed like the back of a duck, and stained brown-green from manure, echoing against the polished wood floor. To the old ones it sounded like the hooves of horses as he crossed the room straight as a plow furrow, shoving aside the folding chairs, the display of purple gladiolas, clearing a path to the open casket.

Drawn by the horses' hooves the old folks glanced through the open door, scowled at the debris in the bed of the pickup—the scythe and shovels and picks, the rusted tools, the blackened pots and pans—and tried to fit it into the fiction of their memories. Through the integrity of their confusion they saw him as a disinherited relative, an immigrant, the prodigal son, or a hobo up from the tracks offering a day's labor shucking corn for a bed in the barn and a plate of chicken.

They had seen so much.

*What a godawful mess,* a woman with high, rouge cheeks said; she was frowning and shaking her head. *What is the world coming to anyhow.*

Digger, in his brown suit with the neat white triangle of a handkerchief in the breast pocket, was standing beside the guest book with his hands folded. On his face was that benign, placid countenance that he wore, like a suit, for the occasion. He was lost in dreamy calculations of time—fifteen minutes, he figured, until the benediction, two hours of cleaning up, folding chairs, stripping the table. According to the plan he would be home in time to watch the news and the *Tonight Show* and have a bowl of Neopolitan with chocolate, peanuts, and sliced bananas, if they were still ripe. This heat was hell on bananas. It was hard to keep them ripe. The callus on the ball of his left foot was giving him trouble and his lower back ached. This posture of reverence was a killer. And he had another funeral on Saturday.

He was watching the Reverend Newhart across the room, shaking the hands of the old-timers. His sneakers squeaked on the floor, and he was too eager, too sympathetic to ever penetrate their reserve. He struggled to recall their names, their lineage. The ol' fire and brimstoners were bad enough, Digger thought, but at least they believed in something. These new preachers they sent you were as flimsy as a pine box.

Then Junior intruded on his thoughts like a snake crossing the road.

He cleared a path through the chairs and flowers, and then, as casually as dropping the hood of a car, closed the lid of the casket, stooped to free the wheels, then hunched down and began rolling it across the room as if pushing a stalled car.

As he passed by the mourners, the blue book of *Yin* and the flask of *Yang* protruded from his rear pockets. A dapper old man with a fedora, boutonniere, and cane, clinging to dignity and grace, stepped forward to help. Junior nodded his thanks, touched the bill of his cap, spit on the shiny wood floor, then rolled the casket on toward the door.

Finally, Digger, his dreams of ice cream and the night show vanishing, lurched toward the door, raised his hands like a child trying to stop a train.

But Junior, the momentum of death on his side, rolled the casket through the doorway, sending Digger stumbling to the side, knocking the gladiolas and the guest book from the stand. As Digger straightened and smoothed his tie his eyes darted from the debris on the floor, to the porch and the old truck, then to the front of the room, to the vacant spot surrounded by bright yellow mums beneath the sad eyes of the beseeching Jesus mounted on the wall.

Outside, crushed oil and beer cans rattled in the bed of the truck as Junior cleared a space. He pushed aside the tools, then slid the casket into the bed as casually as a man loading a sofa.

He slammed the tailgate, hopped down and tapped a squatting tire with the toe of his boot; reassured, he spit, hitched his pants, lifted his cap to smooth his hair, wiggled the cap back down into place, then glanced up at the doorway that framed the undertaker and the man of God, who would venture no farther.

He offered a half salute of farewell, flashed that black-tooth grin, then turned his back and ambled to the cab, wrenched open the door, slid in, and with his arm forked out the window just eased away from the porch, across the lawn of the funeral home, rocked gently over the curb and idled out into the street.

He turned west down the cobblestone street under the arching limbs of the elms, passed the tranquil houses and green lawns where children turned somersaults, picked clover and conceived their destinies, and then turned north toward the hills, toward Turk's Bluff.

*That's the goddamnedest thing I ever heard of,* the sheriff said when Digger placed the call.

## III

Up the swathed trail in the fading light of August he bore her up to the place she'd willed. The useless pile of rocks. The useless pile of bones.

He bore her up, wrapped in burlap, like a child to bed, and he spoke to her, like a child, in his own silence without utterance, *we're almost there.* Then to himself, gasping, *we're almost there.*

In the breeze the whistle of a bobwhite rose over the cooing of the doves. The heavy scent of clover and alfalfa swept up from the valley, across the dry pastures then up the wild slope of the hill.

Near the crest he rested, lay her down, and leaned back on a slab of sandstone pocked like a beehive. In the holes were wild seeds, spider webs, and red brackish water. He waved away a fly and lit a cigarette. The rock was cool against his back. It felt good to be doing something. To be doing something in the fading light. To be doing something he could appraise with his eyes, touch with his hands. In the twilight it was a special feeling. Like going to church for some folks.

Leaning forward with his arms on his knees he looked like a gangly raven about to test the air. Grinning, he could feel the wind against his teeth, his tongue, dry against the roof of his mouth. He could taste the wind.

*You conceived a scavenger,* he said, glancing down at her shrouded in burlap at his feet. He tried to imagine her tasting the wind.

Until yesterday all he had known of her was a remote, efficient figure in the kitchen, sweeping crumbs from the countertops into a cupped hand—that reassuring clamber of dishes being stacked or withdrawn from cupboards, and always that embroidered dish towel in her hands as she stared out the kitchen window at what seemed to a child empty, dry space or the tedious landmarks of barns and windmills, corrals and pastures. He hadn't seen then how she molded that towel, squeezed it and wrung it as her eyes narrowed. *Clean up, now,* she would say in a voice as remote as the wind. *Clean it all up.*

Then yesterday in the granary he discovered her recipe box among the pots and pans, and there among the ingredients for the bread puddings and layered cakes and casseroles were the evocative, cryptic notes: *saw W. J. last night . . . it rained . . . Buck was gone . . . W. J. came . . . brought cin. (sin?) rolls to Will . . . ate them all . . . feel ripe today . . . belly like the mirror of the moon.*

There in the old granary among the stench of mice and moldy seed, oil and dust, he'd cupped that tiny wooden box as if it were a gift, and then his hands began to tremble. A stutter, now, in his hands, too.

He wet a finger and rubbed a stain from the painted rose on the lid, then wiped the box against his pants. A scent of maternal flesh, bath powder and perfume, came to him out of memory, then some other scent, musky and deep and mysterious; the notion of laying his mother to rest where she had enjoyed her illicit bliss, where he himself perhaps had been conceived, fathered by a man more unknown and remote than his own father, rose with the quiet inevitability of the sun. It was something to do with his own life, a way if not to redeem it, then at least leave a memory behind, a story, or at least a damn good outrageous joke. And, nowadays, it seemed, that's all that was available.

So he'd picked up the scythe and cleared a path where she had walked, across the pasture, over the sagging fence, and up the slope of Turk's Bluff. *Clean it up,* he thought. *Clean it all up.*

Now, on the hillside, waiting for his second wind with his hands folded and his head bowed, he spit near a red ant skittering back and forth with a grain of sand twice its size.

*The world ain't built straight, is it. It ain't built on the plumb.*

Down slope to the east the town was beginning to stir. Lights burst out from under the trees, flickered and pulsed on the streets.

Even now the valley looked like it had been forged by the belly of a whale gliding east to west along the soft bottom of a sea, furrowing up rock and silt to form the hills. To the south, the deeper channel of the river was concealed under the corridor of cottonwoods and willows. The precise grid of roads and symmetrical fields looked like linoleum laid over the valley floor. A tractor crept back and forth, sending up its blue plume of diesel smoke as it altered the color and texture of a field. From the east, a train, sounding like a distant rumble of thunder, probed the darkening valley. On the blacktop and gravel roads the wedge of car lights closed on the town. Near the farmhouse and outbuildings blue mercury lights came on and hovered near clusters of shadowy trees. The encroaching darkness obscured the grid of roads and straight rows of corn, beans, and sorghum.

Junior had always felt safer at night. The darkness came without obligation. At night there was a certain grace in silence. He put out his cigarette, rose, and again bore her up.

*C'mon, mom,* he said. *Time to get you planted. They're comin' after us.*

A half hour later he was on top of Turk's Bluff, in a semicircle of sandstone boulders where the cheat grass was dry and brown. He lay her down and found the shovel and pick and scythe where he'd left them earlier in the day.

A yellow half-moon rose over Paradise, over his left shoulder, as he broke ground. The shovel sliced through the webbed roots of the grass, sparked against the rocks near the surface. He pried them loose, piled them separately for later use, then down a foot or two, the digging was easier, the soil sandy until he entered the grave himself and flung the dirt up toward the night sky.

Above him the sky deepened, rolled back into a higher charcoal canopy that made the stars seem closer and brighter than before.

Soon the moon was overhead, and coyotes yapped from the pastureland in the north. A screech owl whistled, fell silent, whistled until its voice faded out into a haunting tremolo.

He sat down in the bottom of the grave to rest. His foot ached under the instep, and sweat burned in his eyes. He was panting, and his arms and face were coated with the silt of the grave. His wet shirt was stretched tight across his back, and his jeans were moist and stiff.

Sitting there, cross-legged, he absorbed the cool air down deep as he smoked and looked up at the sky framed by the grave. There was only darkness and silence and the beauty of the random stars. The night sounds did not reach him. They did not travel down here; they rose to the heavens, apparently, rather than fall, like water, into the hole. His own heavy breath was amplified in the grave. He couldn't see the lights gathering in Paradise. He didn't know they were coming.

Finally his breath slowed, and the sweat evaporated from his brow as he picked up the shovel. His hand was already callused and curved, molded to the handle. *How deep does a man have to go,* he wondered, slicing down through the bottom, then flinging it up over the top. *How deep does he have to go to do it right?* The dirt was beginning to tumble back down. It was a good question, he thought, throwing the next shovelful higher, up over the mound beside the grave. A damn good question.

So he dug deeper, another foot or two, lost in his own labor and silence, until finally he gave it up and told himself it would have to do. *It would have to do.* Then pulling himself back up to the surface of the earth, to the odors of cultivated fields and the night sounds from the pastures, fields, and towns, from man and beast, it occurred to him that if you could still save yourself it probably wasn't deep enough.

The rich scent of clover and alfalfa and ripe corn was overpowering. The fertility a burden. The lights in the farmhouses, the sparkling clusters on the valley floor, the car lights streaming along the roads, turning at right angles, then finally fusing with the lights of Paradise itself intruded on the moment. They made him edgy. He jabbed the shovel into the ground. The engines droned in the darkness—all the irrigation pumps, oil wells, cars, and trucks sounded like the hoarse rumblin' of the surf from an unseen ocean.

*Where were the coyotes?* he wondered. Even they had ceased their yelping. He imagined them lying in wait, crouching in ravines, panting behind thickets in the northern hills, waiting for the drone of engines to pass so they could once again shoot their voices to the stars, reclaim the night.

As he stood up he glanced down at the valley, at the beads of car lights stringing out on the road like a fuse burning toward the hill, and managed a weak ironic smile. *What did ol' Hank say, dying of tuberculosis? Stopping abruptly in the middle of I Saw the Light? That's the problem. There ain't no light,* he said.

Then, stooping, he picked her up, cradled her again in his arms and laid her on the lip of the grave; entering the grave himself, he brought her down, left her there, and escaped to finish his labor. From his pocket he pulled some of the recipe cards that he'd found in the granary, and scattered them in the grave like flowers, hers to take with her into the other life, if luck would have it. There might be a place in heaven for some good chicken gravy.

Who knows, maybe St. Peter admitted those who had the best recipes, the best secrets to tell, the richest inner lives. Silence, then, would be next to Godliness. Wasn't God himself silent? He spit in his hands, picked up the shovel and worked quickly to stave off reflection and the encroaching lights from town.

The first shovelful of dirt thumping against the burlap at the bottom of the grave was the coldest sound he'd ever heard. He closed his eyes, picked out the night sounds of cicadas, the scent of clover, anything but the scrape of his shovel and the cascading dirt into the grave. Rather than tears he offered his sweat; it dripped from his forehead, coursed down his cheeks as he shoveled and scraped, panting, until a rounded cornice arose and he piled the rocks over the mound and struck the handle of the scythe in the loose dirt, angrily, like a warped one-armed cross, then collapsed, spent, beside the grave to await the light.

## IV

The procession of car lights emerged, unsheathed, from the yellow lights of Paradise, headed west on the blacktop, then turned at a right angle, north, toward Turk's Bluff.

The throbbing red light of the sheriff's car led the way, followed by the empty hearse; along the way, remote porch lights and yard lights burst through the night, and pickup trucks bounced down long, rutted driveways to join the procession of light. The drone of engines and the crunch of gravel sounded like the whir of locusts from another time. The background sounds of the night, cicadas and bullfrogs, vanished as the procession of light finally linked the town to the distant, wild hill. The red light splashed against the base of Turk's Bluff, the siren wailed, stopped, echoed somewhere in the distance, and then the dust from the procession rose like smoke from a prairie fire.

For a moment the dust obscured the car lights as they fanned out like soldiers along a skirmish line at the base of the hill. Doors, trunk lids, and tool boxes screeched open and slammed shut and then abruptly the car lights vanished, and a swarm of flashlights cast their disparate beams up and down the hill. Behind the flashlights vague shapes and silhouettes clamored, swore, and grumbled until a single, pleading voice rose above the discordant noise, demanded order and purpose, and it was so.

The solitary lights merged into a single file that began snaking its way up the hill, up the swathed trail that Junior himself had cut, where forty years ago Aggie had sought the freedom of the night, where centuries before Coronado had sought Cibila and then, disillusioned, executed the Turk, where earlier still sentinels of Pawnee and Sioux searched for bison grazing in the tall grass nurtured by the silt from the Permian sea.

Now the yellow, brittle weeds of August bent and snapped under the feet of farmers and businessmen. Soft stone crumbled into powdery sand under their feet. Loose rock tumbled down the slope as their flashlights shot toward the sky, circled the summit, probed the ground for footholds, flickered against the shadowy patches of yucca and sumac and over the listing cedars in the niche.

Above them, still in the darkness, Junior watched and waited, anchored in place by the same stubborn integrity of his immigrant ancestors who defied the evidence. He sat cross-legged, rocking back and forth beside his mother's grave as the lights ascended. He sipped from the flask of Ancient Age, humming *I Saw the Light* as if in a trance, awaiting a vision.

The first flashlights neared the summit, then vanished under the outcropping of sandstone before bursting out on top of the hill, thirty yards away. The men stayed on the trail, but their lights skittered from boulder to boulder, from shrub to shrub, like nervous moths, until one by chance seized him out of the darkness.

*There he is, by God!* a voice rang out.

And then the other flashlights mounting the hill, one by one, honed in on him until he had to close his eyes to preserve the night.

*Shit, it's nothin' but a goddamned shadow,* another voice said.

*Hell, no. It's him by God. It's him.*

*You can't see shit for shinola.*

*I guess I know flesh and blood when I see it.*

In their lights they saw him under the gleaming blade of the scythe as a dark vulture, hunched over the grave, or an aboriginal moaning a death song, someone who had slipped into a silence deeper than their own; and when he raised his head and lifted the flask as if offering a drink to the boys, a voice in the crowd said, *Hell, he's gone off the deep end for sure.*

Then Digger stepped out from the swarm of lights, his brown suit heavy with sweat and his loafers scuffed from the climb. Dry spears of cheat grass stuck to his trousers. He panted as he rattled the sheaf of papers like a sword.

*Goddamnit, there's a law, Junior,* he panted. *There's a goddamned law in this state. You just can't go plantin' folks wherever you damn well please. On some godforsaken useless pile of rocks for just any damn flimsy reason just to suit your own damned self!*

A low rumble of voices behind him assented as the flashlights bobbed up and down. The sheriff's hand snapped at the flap on his holster, and the handcuffs on his belt rattled as he came up beside Digger.

*Hell, Junior. Digger's right. There's a law. There's a proper place, down by the church, all laid out for these kinds of deals.* He paused, then shined his flashlight up to the sky, swept it from horizon to horizon, as if reassuring himself of the universal order, that nothing in the heavens was amiss. Then he aimed it again at Junior as his voice softened, pleaded.

*Hell, I know a man gets carried away ever now and then but, hell, ya know, Digger can't be slighted in this deal. A man can't go off half-cocked like this.*

Junior, his eyes still closed, rocked back and forth as he uncapped the flask and took a drink. Then the Reverend Newhart stepped out of the crowd, joined the undertaker and the sheriff.

*Junior,* he said softly in his somnolent voice. *Let's talk about this. About your loss.*

*Shit, he can't talk,* Digger said, slapping the papers in his palm.

A sweat, different from the sweat of labor, burst from Junior's brow. It stung like thorns. A hot, prickly heat that evoked swarms of vague images of times when he was called on to speak, but couldn't—when he felt the heat of eyes upon him, when his own breath betrayed him. His blood thinned as if pouring into his chest, rising up into his throat behind an impermeable dam of silence. It swelled inside him, engorged by the very desire to speak of it, to open a channel that flowed through the heart, that flowed through time. He wanted to speak for the dumb. He wanted to speak for the dead.

When he began to tremble, he reached down to the loose dirt of the grave. He felt the granules between his fingers, rolled them, and let them fall. It was such a small disturbance on the hill. In memory he heard dishes sliding together in the cupboard, smelled flesh and bath powder, saw a woman's eyes lost in the mystical distance.

He opened his eyes and held his hands up to the light, turning them over and over as if they were a gift, something just given to him, yet he knew their range of calluses, the story behind each nick and scar, their lines that curved, veered, and vanished. Lifelines.

Out of the darkness behind the sea of bobbing lights, Digger's voice rose: *The hell with it. Apprehend the son of a bitch.*

The sheriff drew his pistol. His boots crushed the dry grass as Junior's hands flared, like a magician's sleight of hand, looped through the light bearing in, and then seemed to pluck a card from the air, showing it to the crowd, the sheriff, his witness, as he turned it over in the light, showing both sides, as if to prove that it was what it was before it exploded into a dove that would fly away. He was grinning, and his black tooth looked like a hole in a white fence.

The sheriff, trained to be wary, squinted, leaned closer, affixed his beam on the card.

*Hell, it's just a damned recipe card,* he said.

Then Junior flicked a kitchen match with his thumb. A hiss and small blue flame looked like it burned from his clenched hand as he brought the card and flame together.

The fire flashed up the side of the card as he held it to the breeze; bending to the ground he tucked the card into a clump of cheat grass and folded the dry spears over the tiny flames.

The tinder crackled as the card curled, blackened and disintegrated, then burst into an orange knee-high flame that zigzagged east, ten, twenty, thirty feet, then forged south, down the slope like jagged orange teeth.

At first the sheriff stomped at the low flames, but they snaked away under his boot and leapt up beside him. He whirled, turned toward a larger flame, then finally shielded his face and retreated. Digger grabbed the shovel of a man in the crowd, crouched and tried to smother the flames, but the fire surged across the south face of the hill, and then dark smoke rolled up like a thunderhead over the hill.

A tongue of fire found the clump of cedars in the niche, exploded, launching a pillar of flame into the black canopy of smoke. The men, who had been slapping at the flames with shovels and damp shirts, backed off, grimaced against the heat, coughed, and discarded their flashlights as they scrambled over thistles and stone, down the swathed trail to their cars and trucks at the bottom.

Near the barbwire fence they labored at a fire line as the sheriff called for a tanker. In Paradise the folks who had remained stood on their porches and marveled at the orange glow of the flames, the pillar of dark smoke stretching to the sky, the thrill of the siren, and wondered if it would make the news.

Alone behind the wall of flames Junior watched the red eye of an ember float and dip against the dark sky until dying and turning into ash. He was covered with ash and soot. His eyes burned, and the taste of the charred land was in his mouth, but north of the fire he was safe, and there, to the north, a broad, serene night opened under a clear sky.

He opened and closed his hands, milking the air, then brushed them together as he stood up, straightened and lifted his arms, stretching to the sky. He left the scythe, a one-armed cross, to mark the grave, but returned the flask and blue book to his pockets and used the shovel as a walking stick as he crossed the bluff, circled an outcropping, descended through a chimney of iron sandstone, then entered the grass low on the north slope.

Behind him, south of Turk's Bluff, the din of voices, the flashing lights and orange flames, all receded as he wove his way deeper into the ancient amphitheater of cicadas and darkness until the circle closed around him. He had crossed boundary lines, fences, and furrows under the soft light of the moon and the unfathomable stars. He had dipped down into gullies, scrambled up their slick, eroded sides and then blended with the vague shadows of the night.

He leaned into the breeze, into the damp odors of that fertile stasis and pulled his cap low. The silt of dust and ash, the work of his hands, had turned him into the simple hues of the night. The grass thickened, spires lashed across his arms and hands. Spindly stalks, heavy with seed, whisked against his legs as he sought a song, a sentiment to replace the testament of light.

He couldn't sing, but he could hum, and for a man without illusions, humming was a pretty good deal. Amen, he grinned, as he yielded to that night-sea of grass. Amen.

# About the Author

Richard Lundquist divides his time between the Smoky Valley near Lindsborg, Kansas, and Boise State University in Idaho, where he teaches writing and literature.

2057 042

DATE DUE

171